MW00942584

The Bust

(Live By The Gun Die By The Gun)

An Urban Tragedy Novella by:

Stanley James II

No Brakes Los Angeles
BOOKSTORE
8760 s. Broadway
Los Angeles, Ca 90003

Copyright © 2017 by No Brakes
Published in the United States by No Brakes
Publishing

PUBLISHER'S NOTE

This is a work of fiction. Names, character, places, and incidents either are the product of the author's imagination or are used fictitiously. Any resemblance to actual persons, living or dead, events, or locales is entirely coincidental and not intended by the author(s)

THE BUST   STANLEY JAMES II

The Bust

(Live By The Gun Die By The Gun)

"Ayyee, crip, who called the shuttle buses, and pass the dutchie while you're at it. Yeah, whatever, cuz."

"Everyone down, everybody down, down, lay down, lay the fuck down. Sheriff's Department, bSheriffs. Get your bitch asses down!"

As Tristan tries to make a quick run around the side of the house, tossing a pair of balled up socks onto the side of Mitch's house as he tries to get away, but is welcomed by the barrel of a state issued 9mm pointed directly at his dome.

"My son, my son, my kid is in the house!" pleaded a wide eyed Mitch who looks like a deer who's caught in the headlights.

As Mitch is being thrown to the ground, with his knees caved deeply into his chest from the

4

swarming Gang Task Force of Sheriff's in green also known as the Turtle Squad. The turtle Squad swerved up on them, unnoticed, and hopped out of four white unmarked undercover vans that could be seen gathering up earlier. They were waiting about half a mile away for their go ahead from headquarters. The unmarked vans occupied a total number of sixteen specially trained Sheriff's that made up the Compton, Lakewood, and Long Beach joined Sheriff's Gang Task Force.

The streets of Long Beach was once a good place to live and raise a family. As in time, the city gradually turned into the old Wild Wild West. It was overrun by gangs, drugs, prostitution, and corrupt officials. The employment percentage was at a record low and most residents were fed up, out of money, and couldn't come up with a solution.

The local gangs and cliques that were causing destruction and terror were those of Brick Boyz Crips, Andy Bloc Crips, Mafia Crips, Hood Crips, 2 Naughty and Nasty also known as N2, and

Square Hood Crips. The rate of criminal activity was at its highest peak. It's a kill or be killed type of doggy world.

Death took its toll. Seems as if hell's gates were opened up and all the devil souls were set loose to run the streets that were considered gangbangers and jackers.

"Handcuff every one of these fucking black bastards that call themselves Square Hood Crips," said Deputy Boxer.

The Turtle Squad swarmed in like sharks on their badly hurt prey. They had their state issued 9mm Beretta handguns and M-16 rifles pointed directly at every breathing soul that was outside that afternoon.

You can feel the intensity and tension in the air as neighbors from left, right, and across the street started coming outside to see what was all the commotion about. When everyone found out that it was Mitch's crib that was being raided, they decided to make their way over and be nosey.

"Search them for any weapons or drugs, then sit their black asses on the curb," said Lieutenant J. Thurman who just recently made head Lieutenant of the Gang Task Force 6 years ago. "Search every room, every crevice, every food container that's in the kitchen cabinets. Everything, even the peanut butter jars while I get some information from these fucking bastards."

"Okay, sir," replied one of the officers as he escorted the team through the front entrance of the house in a tactical single file line.

"Man, what the fuck is going on?" said a dismayed Roddy who had to be restrained with two sets of handcuffs due to his large body frame.

Roddy, who stood at 5'11 and weighing around 240 pounds, mostly fat from good eating every night from the finest restaurants all over town. Roddy was that nigga who passed for nearly 1.5 million dollars back in the day when he was a teenager and never looked back. He was considered one of the OG's. He spent his whole life building his cocaine empire, brick by brick, freeway by freeway. Roddy had all of Los Angeles, Arizona, Washington, and St. Louis sewed up. He was like the hood Chapo to some.

Roddy had set up shop and placed some of his homies out there to serve and get money for their organization. He helped a lot of family and friends out by giving them jobs and opportunities, instead of having to go through the white man. Roddy, who just came home from Kern Valley State Prison two months prior after doing seven year prison bid on weapon and money laundering charges. Roddy was known around for having the longest run in the dope game that spanned a little over 20 years.

While everyone laid face down either on the sidewalk or grass, handcuffed. Except for Mitch's oldest sister, Jasmine. She was there standing few yards back, holding her nephew Nasir who was in complete total shock.

As the second in command, Deputy T. Boxer led the rest of the Sheriff's into the blue single story house with a blueprint layout of Mitch's father house in his hands. Mitch's father house was located in the center of the block on Scott Street and Long Beach Blvd., which was centered in the heart of Square Hood turf. Their turf had expanded about a 5-mile radius north and south, which was pretty big for a hood on the Northside.

The Sheriff's stormed in, breaking all doors down, with their sledgehammers, that was in the house. They were tossing and turning over everything that was inside and insight. Purposely breaking Mitch's other MAC laptop computer that was sitting on the living room sofa. They put cracks into his 72' inch flat screen TV that was hanging up on his bedroom wall. They figured that was more than enough damage they had done.

From outside, everyone could hear Deputy Boxer and his team in the house flipping over bedroom mattresses, dumping out all of the drawers

9

onto the floor, and kicking things over. They were going through their house like a wild tornado.

"Is there anything in the house that I should know about?" asked Lieutenant Thurman.

"We don't have shit to talk about and there ain't shit in the house either," Mitch spat as he was laid faced down on the ground handcuffed and confused, still knowing that they were in there damaging his personal goods.

"Yeah… okay, that's not what I hear about you and the company you keep," replied Lieutenant Thurman with sarcasm in his tone.

"It's some nice expensive vehicles here on this street," said one of the Sheriff's while holding perimeter.

"Yeah, so who's the owner of that expensive white Bentley Coupe with the panoramic glass top, and this new BMW that's sitting on some nice expensive rims?" Lieutenant Thurman sarcastically asked.

"Aww, mane… that's mine, Officer," said Roddy with a huge cracked grin on his face. He knew it made authorities mad when they saw black males with nice expensive cars, jewelry, and homes. "Nice, huh?" Roddy shot back sarcastically, knowing that it would make their blood boil for being such a smart ass.

"Man, I'm in the wrong business I see. I couldn't even afford these cars just on my yearly salary alone. What yall do for a living?" the Lieutenant asked, which in back of his mind I knew he clearly already knew we were drug dealers.

"Maybe I need to get into business with yall," said Lieutenant Thurman."Yall some kind of rap group? Wait, wait a minute, I got it. Yall must have an entertainment company or some sort, ain't that what yall gangstas into now a days?" chimed in Deputy Boxer, laughing under his breath.

"I've been hearing a lot of talk about this No Brakes Publishing and Entertainment Movement that's been the talk in these LA streets," he also added laughing with humor.

"Man, fuck all that, do my sister have my baby before y'all conduct your business?" Mitch, who lived at the resident with his father and two older sisters, asked while handcuffed, sitting on the curb with the rest of his homies as he's getting agitated.

"He'll be fine and yes she has him," an unknown female sheriff replied. Mitch couldn't identify the sheriff due to her tactical gear and mask that was covering all of her face.

"Fucking racist, bitch," Tristan spat underneath his breath while spitting out dirt and grass from his mouth.

Every Crip member out there was totally stunned and confused on what was happening. However, raids like this were common in the hood. Running from the police was like exercise to these young thugs.

"This all happened way too fast," Mitch thought silently to himself while shaking his head in shame.

"We found nothing, sir. Only thing we found were these 38. shells that were on the side of the house," said a Deputy as the last of the Sheriff's we're exiting Mitch's ramshackle house.

All all the doors seemed to be barely hanging on to their hinges due to their tactical sledge hammer that they used to break down each door.

"That's impossible," Lieutenant Thurman said, who was now turning cherry red in his cheeks. "Son of a bitch," Lieutenant Thurman mumbled clearly. Of all things, Lieutenant Thurman hated to be lied too, especially about big time drug busts. That could mean a possible promotion and raise for him.

Thurman was a 40-year Veteran that worked the streets of Compton, Lakewood, and Long Beach, which he knew now all so well like the back of his old aged experienced hands. Lieutenant Thurman saw many generations of gangstas come and go with their kids following right into their footsteps, and so on. Many pimps, hustlers, and gangsters around Los Angeles County knew about Lieutenant Thurman and his dumb witted partner, Deputy Boxer. They were known as The Hit Squad because if they're coming for you, they're coming strong and hard. Lieutenant Thurman came from a family bloodline of Military and Corrections Officer's. He was an Army brat that came to LA when his father got a job as a Corrections Officer for the Penitentiary Old Folsom, after being discharged from the Marines.

Lieutenant Thurman, a well hardened officer, went strictly by the book, due to working in the Los Angeles County Jail for 10 years, dealing with every kind of gangster there ever was to walk.

Unlike Sheriff Boxer, who played by his own rules and was compared to Alonzo from Training Day because of his shady ways, and being crooked as can be. He didn't care about anyone other than his own kind and that was the motto he went by daily. He was somewhat new to being on the Gang Task Force. He'd only been with them for only about a year in a half. He had been an officer of the law for only 3 years in total on the force.

Boxer tried to show his toughness by abusing his badge and authority. Many residents hated the way Deputy Boxer conducted his business. Meanwhile, former Crip now turned Federal informant, Junebug, was the only name running through Lieutenant Thurman's head. Junebug was the one that ratted out Mitch who once was from the same set. But it was Mitch who had the hood spotlight and Junebug hated and envied everything about Mitch.

Junebug was eight years older than Mitch and once upon a time, in Crippin history, it was rumored that the two of them were once roll dogs in the upcomings of a young Mitch. As the years went by, real eventually recognized real, and Junebug exposed himself to be a fraud and buster. The streets recognized quickly and Mitch had cut all ties from him for good. Word spread quickly on the streets that Junebug was a hood hopper in his early years of banging. Hood hopping always ended up meaning death and dishonor to any real gang member. Junebug then followed up with snitching on a couple of dudes around the city for a lesser sentence in a drug case he caught four years ago.

Mitch, Tristan, Roddy, and a few other gang members from allied sets around the city knew Junebug's biggest secret that he kept trying to hide and cover up through his macho tough man act. He was a homosexual who slept with other men, quiet as kept. His ex wife, Teresa, was the one who put Junebug out there publicly. Ever since the night she walked in on Junebug and another gangsta named Jo Jo together, butt naked in the bed when she came home from work early.

"Well, look, guy's, before I let you all go, I need to take information, take pictures of your tattoos, and capture you all on video for my records," Lieutenant Thurman growled.

"This some bullshit right here," snarled one of the members in Mitch's crew.

"Some bullshit, huh?" said one of Lieutenant Thurman's men with a cat eye on all the crips handcuffed sitting on the curb in a parallel line. "We know what's going on in the hood. We know what the streets are saying. We know who's who and who's doing what," said Deputy Boxer who was Second in Command on the Gang Task Force.

"So, what does that mean?" Roddy asked bluntly.

"Are we free to go?" Mitch asked.

"Yeah, everything checked out. We came out empty handed. No warrants or anything, but Tristan has to go. We found some shells close to his possession, located on the side of the house, in some socks, balled up. Other than that, all of yall fuck heads are free to go. Oh, and by the way, don't

17

get caught slipping out here in these streets, blood," Deputy Boxer chuckled with vengeance in his voice. He knew it would agitate them because theywere crip members to the core. He knew that there wasn't and never were any bloods in Long Beach. He knew Long Beach was an all Crip city and the only all Crip city in the world, ever since the beginning of gang banging.

"Man, fuck yall! Yall ain't shit without that gun. Yall just some pigs behind some plastic badge with guns!" yelled Blake, one of Mitch's homies who was there earlier, smoking.

"I hear that Deputy Boxer loves setting niggas up against each other to increase gang violence between hoods to make their job easier." He also added under his breath, whispering to Mitch sitting besides him, "We gonna bail you out if necessary."

Mitch hand signaled to Tristan who was handcuffed in the backseat of a squad car, sweating bullets because he already had two strikes and his third would send him away for life.

Tristan was an experienced OG from their set who had been through it all and done it all. To this day, Tristan has always been Roddy's right hand man due to them being close in age. Tristan walked that walk and talk that talk.

"Can I get that search warrant that you still haven't gave me yet?" asked Mitch.

"Yeah, I almost forgot, here it is," Lieutenant Thurman threw it out into the street from the van window. He sped off with the following squad vans and Tristan, on his way to the Lynnwood station.

"Fuck them bitches, they don't have shit on us," echoed Mitch. He was rubbing his wrists. They were swollen due to the overtight handcuffs that cut his wrists.

"You know this won't be the end of this shi,t it's only the beginning," murmured Roddy.

THE BUST

STANLEY JAMES II

Oct 22nd 2013

4:30 am

Earlier that morning

"Yo, what up, murda, you sleep? Backwoods and coffee early morning," asked Roddy with a slight chuckle.

"Naw, I'm up. What's the deal?" shot back Mitch.

"I got some work for us, little cuz.

"I'll be over there shortly, no doubt, homie.

"See if you can get in contact with Tristan, he probably sleep, cuz not answering his cell," said Mitch.

"Shit, that nigga ain't sleep, he been to the pen just like me. We wake up early and besides, I'm surprised that you up this early, nigga," Roddy chuckled.

"Ha, you got jokes, huh, murda. I be up, these are my workout hours," Mitch laughed as he hung up his cell phone.

"Who's that callin you at this time of the morning, baby?" Mitch's baby mother, Amber, asked as she was woke up by Mitch's voice on the phone.

Amber was the definition of a brown skin Queen, someone who stayed down, weathered the storm. She was a real ride or die who had stuck with Mitch through the thick and thin. She stood at only five-foot-four, weighing only 140 pounds. She was brown skin complexion, one that matched one of those aArican Goddesses. She'd first met Mitch when they were in high school. They met through some mutual friends.

Around that time, hanging with Mitch day and night, somewhere down the line Amber fell desperately in love with Mitch. She fell in love with him because of his persona his gangsterism, and most importantly, his ambition. She even loved his drive for the money. He was a true definition of a go-getter. That's what led to their first child, a baby boy seven years later named Nasir.

"It's alright, it's only Roddy, babe. We're baout to handle some business. Start at it early, baby. Go ahead and get your rest and go back to sleep, I'll bring you some breakfast."

"Okay, baby," Amber replied and laid back down.

As Mitch went into the bathroom to run him a soothing hot shower, he turned on his JBL speaker and turned on Pandora. The sounds of Kendrick Lamar and The Game "On Me" blared through his speaker.

After his shower, he got dressed in his typical style of dress attire. The usual dark colored theme button up Polo shirt, gold plated Jesus piece that dangled from his 21' inch franco chain. His True Religion fitted jeans accompanied his green and brown Ralph Lauren Polo boots. His Gucci

Cologne and iced out Bulova watch completeled his fit.

Mitch then headed to the adjacent room. His adjustment room was something like his mini office where he conducted most of his business and got his writings and studies done. He sat at his desk. He then opened and powered on his Samsung laptop as he looked at his son's baby picture that hung above him on the wall. As his laptop proceeded to power on, he did what he he had done every morning. He twisted two fat, honey Dutch Masters of that Diablo OG. It reminded him of Louisville Slugger Bats that his OG homies always did.

He started on the story he previously started writing two year's ago, in hopes of getting it read by some big time publisher in Los Angeles or New York. He had hopes of being signed to a powerhouse publishing company. Although Mitch was perceived as a gangsta and mid-level drug dealer of the streets of Long Beach, Mitch was more than that. He was well educated, very handsome, and charming. He stood approximately five nine in height, weighing 160 pounds wet. He had brown skin and waves that would have any woman seasick if they stared at his hair too long. He was family oriented and most of all, ambitious.

Mitch was always book smart, due to him educating himself solely off of reading all different kinds of books. From Donald Goines to K'wan Foye, Terry L Wroten, Silk White, Kwame Teague, JAquavis Coleman, and William Shakespeare. But Mitch always wanted something more. Something that could change his life and his family's lives in a more legit way. Writing was really the only thing he knew, besides being involved in the street life and dope game.

Mitch was very much different compared to the rest of his homies, but yet he still shared some similarities and traits. Mitch, a couple of year's back, sat down and wrote out his business plan, his goals. Outside of his street life, he wanted to be known as one of the best National African

American Best-Sellers coming from the West Coast, precisely Long Beach. Seeing his name and title on a book in the library, and every time he ended up at Barnes and Noble every other weekend, was something he always seen himself being capable of conquering. Besides, he knew that the street life would always be in him, but he knew that it would eventually come to a complete end.

Mitch snapped out his thoughts when he started surfing through his emails. As he was scrolling, hr came across an email from Terry L. Wroten. He messaged him eight months ago regarding his manuscript and possibly mentoring him into the right direction. Eight months later, here he was, he had Terry L. Wroten responding back and agreeing to look over his manuscript. Simply because Mitch reminded him of an young African American street author and poet of the same degree. He said he saw the same drive in his eyes as he saw in Stanley BabyFace James II eyes.

Mitch sunk deeply into his leather chair. He felt relieved and accomplished about another brick being laid. He then took another pull from his dutch.

"Damn, of all the bad and terrible things I've done in my life, things are finally starting to give," Mitch thought silently to himself, taking it all in.

Oct 22nd 2013

5:37 Am

"Like foe minutes," Murda Roddy said on his iPhone 6.

"Fo'sho, I'm gone unlock the side door. Just come to the patio," Mitch replied.

"10-4." said Roddy.

In the same token of Mitch left his office to unlock the side door. When Mitch grabbed the doorknob to unlock it, Roddy was already walking through with his childish smile.

"Top of the morning," said Roddy as he entered the patio with a medium sized, black duffel bag in each hand.

Mitch walked in and flicked the lightswitch and passed his big homie the last blunt that he was puffing on.

"Top of the morning crip," said Mitch as his face was already revealing his half cracked smile. He already knew what was in the duffle bags. It was what all three homies pieced up on days previously.

Mitch started rubbing his palms together. He knew that his big homie Roddy had just touched down from meeting his Mexican plug, Rafel, that stayed in the city of Lakewood. Every time Mitch knew money or some sort of success was coming, his palms got itchy and moist.

"Go get some latex gloves, the triple beam scale, the Pyrex pot, and some ice cubes for that nigga Tristan when he gets here," Roddy said as he passed back the Dutch Master. He was coughing uncontrollably while removing his 9mm Beretta pistol from his waistband. He then placed it on the counter. "We have to get an early start before the rest of the homies come through."

"No doubt," said Mitch. "But first, I have to make a run to Denny's and grab my ol lady some breakfast before she goes to work at 7:30."

29

"Bet," said Roddy. "And on the way, grab some hot chocolate and a lot of whip cream because boy, you whipped like a muthafucka, bruh!" Roddy said, breaking out into laughter.

"Yeah, right," Mitch said as he left out with the door and closed it behind him.

Forty-five minutes later, Mitch was pulling his 2010 all black BMW with leather interior, woodgrain grips, and 4G audio, up the driveway. He walked back into the patio, after putting Amber's breakfast in the microwave.

"So, it's a go, huh?" asked Mitch.

"Yep, it's about that time of the month again, homie," said Roddy.

Roddy looked at Mitch like a little brother, just like everyone else in the neighborhood. Everyone loved Mitch, he was something like the shining star that made everyone draw too him. Everyone knew that Mitch was their key to financial freedom. Mitch's eyes told it all about him because of his long thick eyelashes, which the ladies loved.

Their relationship went beyond years throughout their turf. Many days, Roddy picked Mitch and his homies up from school. Roddy stayed, once upon a time, just a couple of blocks from Mitch and Tristan, They all stayed and grew up together on the same street. Roddy, Tristan, and Mitch had all put in work together. So taking a man's life was nothing new.

Tristan's family had owned their house ever since the early seventies. Ten years later, Mitch's family moved a couple of houses down in the mid-eighties. Mitch and Tristan was Roddy's top earners. Hthey were his go-to guys and more importantly, his closest homies that were still left. Only a age gap difference between the generations separated Roddy and Tristan from Mitch and his crew of Tiny Gangsta's known as the TG's.

Mitch and his crew had his hood and certain sections surrounded on lock. Anything and everything that happened within the hood boundaries had to go through Mitch and he had to go through his upper superiors. Any bag of weed being sold to the slightest nickel rock that was pitched on the corner, Mitch knew about it and had a percentage in every transaction that went on.

The block was rolling bring in good amounts of money. Street soldiers were positioned on each corner of the block that they ran, which was in control of Mitch.

"How's the intake been for you?" asked Roddy.

"It's coming along well," Mitch replied. "We're taking in about 10,000 a week."

October 22nd 2013

7:15 Am

"Yall are kind of loud this morning, damn, Mitch."

"Good morning to you too," Roddy spoke.

"Good morning, Roddy" Amber said as she was gathering her work stuff together while putting on her makeup.

"Good morning, baby. How was your sleep?" Mitch inquired, "Oh yeah, your breakfast is waiting for you in the microwave. It's a breakfast burrito with some hash browns from Dennys."

"Thank you, love, Oh snaps, I'm about to be late. Let me get out of here." Amber grabbed her food and kissed Mitch good bye.

"Have a nice day at work," Roddy said playfully as Amber closed the patio door behind her. Her hips were swaying, making her ass bounce each step she took.

"Dog, you have a good woman on your side," said Roddy.

"So, have you spoke to Tristan yet?" asked Mitch.

"Yeah, he said he was walking down here now from his grandfather house." That was only a couple houses down from Mitch.

Knock knock.

"Speaking of the Devil," said Roddy as Mitch opened the patio door to greet Tristan.

"What up, loc? Did it go through? Tristan asked with such urgency in his voice.

"Uh, you know it. Let's get this shit done, cuz. I got some people coming to pick up shortly," said Mitch.

"What we dealing with, anyway?" asked Tristan.

"We got seven bricks that we're all going to split up three ways. Its going to be two a piece and

34

the last of the crumbs we will break-down the middle and split what's left over, cool?"

"Yeah, no problem," the two stated.

Tristan was around the same age as Big Rod, but happened to be the big homie to Mitch who he had helped raise in the same way as his own son. They were all from the same gang but generation gaps were what separated one another.

As Tristan got too cooking, he had the whole room smelling like a strong scent of cocaine.

"Pass me a couple of ice cubes, Mitch," said Tristan who was a pro at cooking dope.

Tristan was the man to come to when it came to whipping and selling dope. He came from the era of where you could turn a fourteen into twenty-one easily with no blow up.

"Who you got coming over for a pick up, anyway?" Tristan asked.

"That punk ass nigga Junebug," shot back Mitch.

"You know it's something about that nigga I don't like, cuz," said Tristan with fire in his eyes.

"Yeah, but fuck it. As long as he brings the dough, I don't give a fuck. Fuck that nigga, he ain't from the set no more, in my eyes," Mitch said.

"Yeah, I hear that but I still don't trust cuz, never have and never will," Tristan said with authority. "But on another note, how is your book coming along, homie?" Tristan asked Mitch who knew everything about him without even asking.

"This is gonna be the one that makes a name for myself in this urban fiction game," said Mitch eagerly. "This book is going to solidify and stamp my signature with all the other great black writers of time. Hopefully after this book, I won't have to ever go back to the corners pitching again, on crip. You feel me?" said Mitch with such sincerity in his voice.

"Yeah, I feel you and believe in you," replied Tristan with Roddy agreeing.

October 22nd 2013

11:27 Am

"Damn, it smell like a Colombian cocoa farm in this bitch," said Julian, jokingly with another younger homie that claimed TG's, from the set.

"What yall got up this morning?" he asked everyone.

"Same shit different day, murda. You know how that shit be," Tristan said.

Both, Mitch and Roddy, came back into the patio after stashing their two bricks. They then gave Julian daps.

"What up, Crip? said Mitch.

They all walked to the front of the resident after they had cleaned up the patio and inspected it like normal routine working days. Since day one, Tristan has always had the mentality to clean up and inspect the work space after cooking a lot of dope. Just prior, he made sure he got rid of all drug paraphernalia in fear of raids by the local authority, in which he had been in plenty of throughout his years of hustling. Tristan has just recently got out of the pen no more than 6 years ago.

"You seen that weird nigga Junebug?" asked Mitch. "He was supposed to be coming to get this half ounce."

"Yeah, as a matter of fact, I seen that nigga at the store while I was getting some Dutch Masters and Back Woods. It looked like he was on his way over here now," replied back Julian.

"Here he is coming down the street now."

At that moment, an old 2006 Chevy Monte Carlo that was two toned burgundy, turned the corner with the sound system squeaking through its blown out speakers.

"What up, little Mitch? I see you still out here doing your thang and all. I see you're writing books, poems, and shit," Junebug said with an envous devilish stare.

"My bitch saw some of your work andsaw your book in that Poets and Writers Magazine. She said, look. isn't that one of your homies, babe?"

"Yeah, I'm still doing my thang," Mitch said concisely back

"Yeah, whatever, homie. You got that for me or what?" an angered Junebug spat.

"Yeah, you got the money?" Mitch hissed back.

"Yeah." Junebug slid the wad of money to Mitch and in the same hand, he slid the half ounce of rock cocaine back.

"This better be all of it," snarled Junebug.

"Don't you still owe me some money, nigga?" Mitch sarcastically said.

Before everyone else that was standing in the background could get a laugh in, Junebug felt embarrassed, especially in front of his lady. Burnt rubber filled the air as Junebug, and his girlfriend that was in the passenger seat, sped away down the block.

"Fuck nigga," Mitch mumbled under his breath as he was still looking at the back of the Monte Carlo speeding off down the street.

"Fuck that bitch ass little nigga, Mitch."

***

"I got a major surprise for him and them bitch ass niggas that still fuck with him," Junebug shouted at his girl. She knew Junebug was a full fledge hater of Mitch and his homies because the hood wasn't claiming him anymore.

"Baby, why you don't like Mitch nomore?" asked Tina, Junebug's girlfriend.

"Fuck that little bitch ass nigga. That nigga haven't did shit, he just picked up where we left off," Junebug hissed at his girlfriend.

They then made their way to the Hit squad's car, It was parked at the laundromat so he could talk to Lieutenant Thruman.

"So, what do you have for us, boy?" asked Deputy Boxer.

"Who the fuck are you calling a boy? You fat bacon wrapped, pig in a blanket," Junebug shot back at him.

"Cut all the games. Now, what do you have for us?" Thruman asked with controlness in his tone.

"An half ounce of rock cocaine from Mitch," Junebug tossed the pre-packaged dope from his window onto Thruman's lap.

"Good, son," Deputy Boxer said with a smile that was a look of him being less than a man.

"So, we straight now?" Junebug asked.

tina sat back listening on theit conversation, trying to nosey as possible.

"We're straight when I say we're straight," Thruman shot back. "Now get the fuck out of here and make me some more money."

"Fucking cock suckers!" Junebug said as the Hit Squad cars drove off.

Who knew hos life was going down the drain. He knew it was just a matter of time until all of his snitching would catch up to him with a bullet to the head.

Junebug pulled back off into traffic and started reflecting on his whole life.

October 22nd 2013

12:43 pm

"Ayyee, Kiewe, who called the shuttle buses and pass the blunt while you're at it. Yeah, whatever cuz."

"Everyone down, lay down. Compton Sheriffs, Sheriffs!"

"My son, my kid is in the house, please!"

"Handcuff everyone search them, and, then sit them all on the curb," said Deputy J. Thurman.

"Search every room while I get some information from these bastards."

"We don't have shit to talk about and there ain't shit in the house either," said Mitch as he was laying eagle spread on the ground.

"Yeah, that's not what I hear about you and the company you keep. So, who's the owner of all these nice expensive car's?" Letinuant Thurman sarcastically asked.

"Aww, mane, those are mine, officer," said Roddy. "Nice, huh," he shot sarcastically back.

"Man, I couldn't even afford those luxuries on my yearly salary. What yall do for a living?"

"Can my sister hold my baby while yall conduct yall search?" Mitch asked while he was handcuffed and sitting on the curb with the rest of his crew.

"He'll be fine," another officer replied.

Mitch couldn't identify the Sheriff due to his tactical gear and mask that was covering his face.

"We found nothing, sir."

The last of the sheriff's we're exiting Mitch's ramshackled house. The door barely hung on the hinges due to the batter ram.

"That's impossible," Lieutenant Thurman said.

Of all things, Lieutenant Thurman hated to be lied too about, money and drug busts. Former gangsta now turned federal informant, Junebug was the only name running through Letinuant Thurman's head. He was the one that ratted out Mitch who was from the same set. But it was Mitch's turn to have the hood spotlight and Big Junebug hated and envied everything about Mitch.

"Well, look guy's. Before I let you all go, I need to take information, take pictures of your tattoos, and capture you all on video for my records," Letinuant Thurman growled.

"This some bullshit right here," snarled one of the members in Mitch's crew.

"Well, if yall have any problems, take it up with my superior. Better yet, with any complaints, write it down on a piece of paper, put in a envelope, and address it to the Compton Sheriff's Department and shove it directly up yall asses," said Leinuant Thruman.

"Fuck you," replied Julian with anger in his voice and fire in his eye's.

11:49 pm

"Damn, what they charged you with, homie?" Mitch asked Tristan. He had took a Taxi from the Sheriff's station. He smelled like the old Lynwood sub station.

"Cuz, they're fishing. They're trying to find something out. All they found in that raid was a box of 38 shell bullets with no gun," Tristan said. He hated the local authorities and always had.

"But, you know what though, loc? someone is working for them boys."

"Yeah, that's the same thing I've been thinking lately," Mitch said.

"The feds been watching for sometime now too?" Tristan added.

"Well shit, it ain't 2 O'clock yet. Atlantic Farms is still open, right there on Atlantic and Artesia. Let's go grab a 5th of Hennessey and some trees," Mitch implied.

It was just Mitch and his big homie Tristan left at the end of the night. The rest of the crew members dispersed and went thir separate ways. Mitch made it to his driveway and stumbled his way into the house. He was drunk and high from the Henny and Platinum OG that he and Tristan indulged hours previous. He turned on the shower and turned on his Pandora and played Nipsey Hussle ''Dont take no days off."

He undressed and placed his wad of bills, something like forty-five-hundred all crisp blue face hundreds, on his nightstand. He then sat his all black rubber grip 44 Desert Eagle pistol next to his gold Franco Jesus piece.

"Damn baby, what happened earlier today? Is everything okay? It's Roddy who they're after, huh?" Amber innocently asked. She was laying up in bed reading her daily word. She was trying to stay awake until she seen Mitch's face before she fell asleep.

"Everything's cool, love. What you doing still up when you have to be at work in a couple of hours? It's good, someone just hating on me. They trying to get me set up in some shit with Roddy but they didn't have anything. So they let us all go. But they took Tristan for them old shells he had and because of the severity of his prison record," replied Mitch.

"Please baby, I know you ain't as half as dumb and crazy as your homies, but be safe baby. We need you," Amber said. Her voice was soft and warming that any man couldn't resist without smiling.

After Mitch took his shower, he laid in bed next to Amber who was already fast asleep. As soon as Mitch leaned over, Amber cradled into his arms romantically. He felt her juices starting to flow, leaving Mitch with a hard on. As things got deeper and sexual quickly, Mitch found himself down south using his tongue to perfection while going up and down working on her clitoris.

Amber woke up wet and warm after feeling the tongue power of Mitch. Her juices ran down her thighs as Mitch ate a mouth full. Not soon after, they were in full scale of sexual activities. Amber then went down on him. She sucked on the tip and made her way all the way to his torso like she was sucking on the corner store pickles. Gagging and spitting on the head of Mitch's dick caused him to precum in Amber's mouth. His toes started to curl.

After laying her down on the bed, he went deeper and deeper he missionary style. He was thrusting all his nine inches of hard dick into Amber. She couldn't help from screaming so loudly and trying climb up the bed.

Mitch then turned her around with her ass up and her face down onto the pillow. That way, she could bury her face into the pillow to help relieve her from screaming so loudly that the neighbors could hear.

"Deeper, daddy, deeper," Amber pleaded while Mitch went deeper with every stroke.

"Who is daddy?" asked Mitch.

"You are, baby. You are, daddy. The one and only," Amber replied in her sexy innocent voice.

After about an hour and a half of inanimate passionate sex, Mitch laid there in complete silence. He stared at the ceiling in the pitch dark room. Amber laid next to him fast asleep and naked. Still on his mind was something that kept drawing him back to what his homie Tristan said earlier.

Junebug…

October 23 2013

7:37 Am

Like clockwork, Mitch was programmed to waking up early around 4 o'clock every morning to he go about his normal routine. He would workout, shower, dress, smoke, and then hit the office to knock out some chapter's for his book so he could finish it and send for editing and review. The sounds on his Pandora speaker was playing the tunes of J Cole "No Role Models."

He sat back and meditated, thinking about life, in general. Before he hit the streets with his right hand man, C Mac. He was also a TG but was four years older than Mitch. He was only the tender age of twenty-two.

Amber had already taken their son to his grandmother's house while she went to work.

Mitch's Galaxy Note 5 started ringing, playing the ringtone of the late rapper Chinx "The Other Side."

"What up, loco?" Mitch answered.

"Come on, nigga. I'm in the front. You ready?" C Mac replied. He seemed to always be turnt up no matter what time of day or location.

"Yeah, right. Here I come, let me grab my Northface jacket," Murda Mitch said before hanging up.

Outside was sitting on a brand new 2011 cream Infiniti sitting on it's original stock rims. Sat a greasy light skin C Mac who was choking while putting out his Backwood into the ashtray.

"Tips," Mitch said as he gave him dap and then fastened his seat belt. "What we on today?" Mitch asked while lighting up a wood that was sitting in the ashtray.

"Shit, we gotta shoot too LA off of Imperial and Vermont and pick these flyers up for our upcoming party that we throwing at Secret Sunday's next month."

"No doubt," Mitch replied while passing the Backwood to C-mac. "Before we hit the 110 freeway, stop at London's Liquor Market on Bort Street so I can grab some more Backwoods, Dutch Masters and some of that Hennessey."

Speeding through traffic, lane to lane, they smashed down freeway while bumping the tunes of Meek Mill "Monster." They were bobbing their heads while reciting his lyrics.

As C Mac pulled his Infiniti into the Arco gas station on Imperial and Vermont, things just seemed odd for the pair. Standing out front were about sixteen young gang members. They were aging from fourteen to about twenty-one years of age. They were just hanging in front of the gas station, looking as if they were from Denver Lanes Bloods from the DLB hats to the red shoestrings and attire they were sporting.

Now a days, in Mitch's time, gang members weren't into the old style gangster dresscode. In LA, the dresscode hadn't changed that much for them.

Hardly ever in Long Beach you would see a rag hanging from a gangsters back pocket or worn on their heads. You would only see white tees and dickie pants. The style on the streets were Robin Jeans, fitted joggers, and Gucci Louis Vuitton everything. The more chains the better.

So happen, on this day with the warm of the sun beaming, both C Mac and Mitch were dressed in blue, showing that they were affiliated with Crips. Mitch was dressed down in his blue button up shirt, with his grey fitted joggers that matched his grey and blue Puma shoes along with his Northface jacket. C Mac was wearing their hood hat, which was the original blue and gold Milwaukee Brewers hat with a Soulja Boy Blvd shirt with some 501 Jeans and his Penny Foamposite.

"Fuck, cuz, what are luck?" C Mac said. He knew he shouldn't have even pulled up to that gas station. He shrugged his head nonchalantly.

"Fuck it, I'm a go pay for the gas," Mitch said. He always stay strapped with his all black rubber grip 44 Desert Eagle pistol that stayed on his hip.

"Yep," said C Mac. He took his personal 9mm glock from his stash that was personally built in his Infinity dashboard. He placed it on his lap while over seeing Mitch as he got out the car and headed to the front door of the gas station.

"What's brackin, blood?" the youngest of the blood gang members said towards Mitch's direction.

"What up, cuz?" Mitch responded with *that try me* nigga look on his face. He walked past and walked into the store.

Mitch stood in line, waiting for the cashier. It was a Mexican lady with her three young kids a head of him. Mitch already knew the rules of the streets and they were out of bounds and slipping. A split seconds like that could cost your life at any given second in the land of scandalous.

After the Mexican lady with her three kids paid and left, Mitch stepped up.

"Can you put twenty-five dollars on pump number five?"

Mitch knew that the bloods from Lanes were going to say something when he walked out. Mitch never feared anything, except his mother. She was the only person in the world that could get to him in a way that no one possibly could. Mitch's Desert Eagle that was already locked and loaded on the side of his hip. It was undetectable, he knew he might have to use it on this day at this gas station. He was was ready for the anticipation. Death was in the air and it was felt throughout the atmosphere.

Mitch walked towards the door. Before Mitch even stepped off the curb he heard one of the bloods shout out, "Aye, blood, where you from again? Because you fasho don't look like you from around here, homie? You must have a death wish or something because this Denver Lanes Blood over here."

"Yep, I know where I'm at. This Long Beach Squarehood Crip on mine, homie," Mitch felt the imprint of his Desert Eagle that was on his hip.

All of the Bloods noticed his gunprint and started shaking their heads.

"Yall know what time it is," said an unfearful Mitch.

All the of Bloods that were standing behind their main shotcaller of the clique started reaching for their pistols. However, before an epic gun battle started, two families pulled into the gas station. One old black family that seemed they were just leaving a church service and the other was a Mexican family that were buying some motor oil for their car that seemed to be giving them problems. Luck seemed to be favor in Mitch's grace when the families pulled into the gas station between the two parties of different cities and different rag colors.

"We can't shoot this crab ass nigga now, cuz. All of all these witnesses and especially these new security cameras they just put up," whispered one of the foot soldiers into the Blood's shot caller ear, named something of Bixyduece.

"Fuck it, you're right. Let's follow this clown ass nigga and catch blood down the street," Bixyduece told his troops.

In the same word, they all hopped in two separate cars. One was an old Buick Regal that had no license plate and the a old 2001 Caprice that was on its way out.

As Mitch made it back to the car, he told C Mac that the Blood niggas were tripping. "Watch these niggas while I pump the gas," Mitch said.

"I'm already knowing," C Mac said. He had his 9mm glock out the stash compartment and resting on his lap.

As Mitch was pumping the last of the gas, he watched both cars sit across the parking structure watching him.

"Oooh, it's another crab ass nigga with him that's driving," Bixyduece said. "We got us a couple of live fish," he smiled while rubbing his hands and palms together. However, he didn't know that death was uncertain and anybody could leave in a body bag on these scandalous streets of Los Angeles.

After Mitch finished pumping the last of gas, he got into the car. C Mac started it up and leaned over. "Yeah, shit about to get real. They trippin, murda," He said with a firm look.

"Yeah, I'm already knowing they gonna follow us until they get close enough to pop," Mitch said.

"Fuck it, cuz. When you pull off, hit straight back to the 110 freeway like you going towards the hood. If they follow us onto this freeway entrance, I'm a let these niggas have it," Mitch said with his pistol in his lap.

"Shit, me too, Crip. You pop your blamer, I'ma pop mine too, nigga. What the fuck you thought this was?"

As C Mac pulled off from the gas station, he banged a right and sped off towards the freeway. Trying to keep up in their old Regal and Caprice, the Bloods managed to get stuck behind two cars that were in front of Mitch and C Mac. It was only one more light to the freeway entrance. Every second counted as time seemed to slow down. The second the light turned green, all Mitch and C Mac heard were the sounds of zipping bullets and glass shattering from the windows of C Mac's Infiniti.

"Duck down, my nigga, they busting at us," said Mitch. "Fuck it, hit the freeway, cuz!" he yelled at C Mac as glass shattered everywhere in the car.

The two cars that were in front of C Mac and Mitch swerved to the far right so they could be out of the way from the brazenness hot bullets that the Bloods were spitting at the Crips car ahead. "Don't let these crabs ass niggas get away!" Bixyduece yelled at the driver of the old beat up Caprice.

"Cuz, as soon as you hit the entrance of the freeway, slow down so I could unload on these fuck niggas," Mitch said with vengeance in his voice.

60

"Here they come tryna swoop on us now," C Mac said while looking from his rear-view mirror. "We got em," one of the blood members said in the back seat. He had a full smile and a smoking gun.

Within a split second, C Mac stepped on the brakes just enough to slow down. Mitch then hung out the passenger window, holding on to nothing but the seat belt. He unloaded all 8 rounds that broke through the Caprice's windshield. The shots hit the driver two times in the chest and once in the neck, killing him on impact. Their shot caller, Bixyduece, he was killed instantly from a single shot to the temple between the eyes.

Following another hail of heavy gun rain, C Mac unloaded all but 12 of his rounds. He tagged the Blood members that were in the Regal. They maneuvered on the side of them, causing the Regal to run and crash straight into oncoming traffic of an Astro Van. In the van was a Latino family with five young children. They caused a great bodily car accident pile up. C Mac's Infiniti was going over a hundred miles per hour down the 110 freeway, heading straight to the hood.

12:15 pm

"Fuck, we killed them bitch ass niggas, huh?" stated Mitch. He was in total shock and dismay.

It had only been a couple of times the two of them went on missions together and shot enemies but never actually killed anyone together. They both had now crossed the fine line into the murder game together.

The duo sat at the Motel 6 hiding out with their ears glued to the scanner. They were seeing what the word on the streets was and trying to catch any unusual police activity lurking.

C Mac's attention went from the window to his cell phone that was ringing. It was his homegirl Tyanna. She stated that a big shootout and car accident that happened not too long ago where they were at in LA getting the flyers.

"You heard or seen anything about that?" asked a nosey Tyanna.

"Word? That happened?" C Mac asked nonchalantly. "Naw, I haven't heard nothing or seen anything," said C Mac.

"Yeah… hold on, my homegirl is telling me more about what's going on now," Tyanna said as she started getting texts messages through her cell phone.

"It's already in the streets," C Mac told Mitch. Mitch was was busy actively listening to his scanner while looking out the window.

"Hello? C Mac, my homegirl said it was some blood niggas. She thinks they're from the Lanes that died. One of them being was a OG reputable named Bxyduece," Tyanna said into the cell phone receiver.

"Oh yeah? Did she say how many people died?"

"Umm yeah, she said it was six people in the shooting and four died. Three were shot to death and one from an crucial car accident involving a Mexican family."

"Did they mention who killed them?" Mitch said in a low tone to C Mac so he could ask Tyanna.

"Did they mention who killed them?" C Mac asked.

"Umm no, they don't know exactly who shot them. But all they do know that it was some Crips from Long Beach."

"Yeah? Damn," C Mac said with a childish grin on his face.

"Yeah, that's why I called you. Knowing well, you know, baby."

"Nah, I didn't see or hear anything. But, good looking out for that info, boo. I'll see you sometime tonight, alright?" C Mac said.

"Okay, baby," she simply replied. "Just call me before you come, so I could get rid of this broke nigga over here," Tyanna hung up her cell phone with a smile on her face.

"Damn, it's already floating through the streets already, Crip," C Mac said to Mitch in a serious tone. "They don't have no names or anything like that, but said it's some niggas from a Long Beach Crip gang," C Mac added, trying to relieve Mitch from any stress. "Shit, we good. Fuck them slob ass niggas," C Mac also added. "Them niggas was asking for it, anyway," C Mac said while twisting up 2 grams into his Backwood.

"Shit, see if the police is even riding through like they should be."

"Hell, people couldn't tell who we were, anyway," C Mac stated. "Now let's go around the corner to the homegirl Kiya house and see if we can find Julian ass somewhere floating around through the hood."

The both of them hopped into C Mac's car and drove around the corner. They didn't tell any of their homies that were posted in the turf about the activities that they were involved in earlier that morning.

They managed to catch their homie Julian walking down the street with three of his cousin's from Lynwood. They were some Squarehood wannabes. They always wanted to get put on the set since their teenage days. Growing up, they watched Mitch, C Mac and their cousin Julian do their thang on the block.

"What up, foe? Who are these niggas you got with you?" C Mac asked. He didn't even recognize them. It had been years that passed since the last time he saw them.

"They're my cousin's from Lynnwood. Yall remember Tyrone and Dee Dee, don't yall?"

"Yeah, I remember them little bad ass niggas since they were kids," Mitch gave each one of them daps.

"Soo, yall wanna be from the set, huh?" C Mac came out and asked.

"Yeah, we do," they both answered together.

"Fuck it, let's go to the hood park, Coolidge Park, up the street and handle our business there."

The party of five made their way to the park. When they got there, they were greeted by several of their big homies. They were standing nearby but behind the restroom area. They were shooting dice, smokin weed while some indulged in smoking PCP and snorting cocaine.

"What up, Mitch?"

"Nothing much," Mitch responded while giving daps.

"What y'all niggas got cracking?" his big homie Tristan said. He had just come from sniffing a couple of lines of powder cocaine.

He was there with his homies that were in his generation, which were the original OG from Squarehood. He really didn't fuck with any TG's due to all the havoc and gang wars caused by those bad ass young bastards who were only trying to make a name for themselves as a reputation. The OG's only talked to Mitch, out of all the TG's because they all felt he had the crown of the younger generation, and he was sharp on both sides of the penny.

"Shit, we have two prospects ready to get put on the turf and we need the green light."

"Shit, I dont give a fuck. That's your thing," another OG by the name of Big Cuz stated as he rolled the dice that he had 20 dollars on. "Seven, mothafucka's, I win. Give me my money," he yelled as he picked up his earnings with a lit newport between his lips.

"Shit, them niggas solid, right?" Tristan asked.

"Yeah, they good soldiers. They're my cousin's, they can hold their own," Julian said. "They just recently moved back to Lynwood from Apple Valley."

"Well, shit, put them on then, fuck it. It's your call," he added in.

With no time wasted, Mitch took the first swing, giving Dee Dee the most fastest overhand right that connected to his jaw. That punch sent him down, crashing to the pavement. Mitch let him get up only to catch him with a quick combination of jabs and uppercuts. The rest of the other TG homies swarmed and rushed Dee Dee and Terone so they have an official put on like wild dogs.

They both were beaten pretty bad. Punches were being thrown left and right. They were fighting like young gladiators fighting for freedom. Terone walked away with a broken nose and Dee Dee walked away with a swollen jaw and bruised ribs due to the heavy blows they were enduring for 60 seconds. But at the end of the day, everyone were homies and that was that no love lost.

Not soon after the put on of Dee Dee and terone, everyone were together indulging in the dice game or tagging their name and hood on the walls to represent.

"Shit… yep, fasho. Fuck it, C Mac, lets hop into traffic and check the traps," Mitch insisted while lighting up a dutchee.

"Yep, we will get with yall another time," C Mac and Mitch said as they were giving all the homies daps and hugs before making their exit".

While it was still early in the day, the two decided to hit the Lakewood Mall and cop a couple of outfits and kicks, something that they usually did.

As Mitch and C Mac were walking through the mall doors, C Mac has noticed a brown cocoa skin ebony BBW that was looking at some pink and black Jordans. Before Mitch could even double take, C Mac had already slid right up on her, shooting game.

"So, those are what you looking to buy, huh, ma? What's your name? As a matter of fact, you look hella familiar." That was the line he used with every girl he came across.

"Ha, you funny, do you use that same line with all your females?" she replied willingly to go along with his game. "And, my name is Rina, what's yours? Is that your brother who's standing behind you?" referring to Mitch. "

"Yeah, that's my cousin Mitch. My name is C Mac, but you can just call me Mac," he was smiling from ear to ear.

"Who you here with, Rina?" C Mac asked.

"I'm here with my soon-to-be ex-boyfriend. He over there getting me some Panda Express."

C Mac looked over and noticed it was Junebug who was standing in line, trying to be unseen. "Damn, like that?" C Mac said with a blank expression.

"Straight like that," she smiled.

Mitch grabbed C Mac's arm. "Yo, C Mac, lemme holla at you for a minute. You know who she is, right?" Mitch asked while looking over C Mac's shoulder.

"Naw, who is she, cuz?" C Mac asked.

"She's that busta ass nigga Junebug's girl. She was with him couple of days ago when he bought that half of brick."

"Yeah, you're right. No wonder she looks hella familiar," he said as he went over her face in his mind.

"Watch that bitch ass nigga," Mitch mentioned. "It's something about cuz, homie. Cuz is a snake.

Before C Mac could go back and holla at Rina, Junebug was already standing on the side of her. He was low key mad, but not trying to show that he knew C Mac was trying to knock his girl. Which in reality, she was feeling his whole get down and gangster demeanor, but trying to play hard to get.

"What y'all little niggas doing up here?" asked a suspicious Junebug with his evil stare.

"Shit, came to buy some fits," C Mac responded while still looking at Rina in her eyes.

Junebug's eyes grew wide when he seen Mitch coming to the line after looking at some shoes. He made his way over and stood next to C Mac at the cashier, purchasing him the new Kobe's.

"Your total is 166 dollars and 36 cents," said the cashier.

"No problem and could you throw in some NBA socks also," Mitch took a wad of blue crisp face hundreds from his back pocket. He counted out two hundred dollar bills. He gave the cashier the money and told him to keep the change.

"Thank you for shopping with us," the cashier said with a grin on his face.

"Oh, you here with this little nigga too?" Junebug said, enviously with venom in his cracked voice.

"Yeah, we're shopping, you know we gotta look fresh so we can take niggas girls and babymommas," said Mitch, who knew he would strike a nerve in Junebug's body.

Before anyone could blink, in that split second, something snapped in Mitch. He jumped on Junebug without giving him a warning. The first two punches that landed had Junebug in a full scale dash out the Foot Locker store. He stumbled like usain bolt. C Mac then tried to get a couple of hits and kicks in. Junebug dashed out the mall, leaving his girl Rina behind and amazed.

"Faggot ass nigga, I swear, when I catch that bitch ass nigga!"

"We gotta get out of here, loco, before the mall security come snatch us up and call the police," C Mac said as he passed Rina a twenty dollar bill with his number on it.

As they hurried and made their exit from the mall, they hopped into C Mac's car and sped off into traffic.

"That's a bitch ass nigga," C Mac added while switching lanes.

"Fuck em, they luckily you got to him before I did, knowing that cuz never liked us, anyway." "Shit, it's still only 3:40, let's pickup some guns and ammunition out there in Palmdale, from one of the homies from the turf," C Mac said.

"No doubt," Mitch nodded as he took the half blunt from the ashtray and relit it. He then took a few drags and then turn up the car stereo, playing Problem's song called *Like What?*.

As the two of them were leaving their homie's crib in Palmdale, they had a trunk full of different kinds of handguns and fully automatic assault rifles. They headed back to the hood to give each homie some steel for protection.

Their vehicle was pulled over as soon as they were exiting off the 91 East freeway exit on Long Beach Blvd, by the Highway Patrol. Loaded and stashed in C mac's trunk were weapons of mass destruction. He had Uzi machine guns, AK 47s, one 223, and a couple of 45's, and 9mm pistols. C Mac personally kept the Glock 17 because glocks were his favorite gun. He knew Mitch loved 45, but his favorite gun was the 50cal and 44 Desert Eagle's. So he got him an all black 50 cal Desert Eagle.

C Mac tossed him his favorite gun into his lap and said, "Merry Christmas, loco," when it was only October.

"My nigga," Mitch said as he was admiring his new strap.

"Shit, the mothafucking Highway Patrol is lighting us up, crip," C Mac said.

"Be cool."

"May I have your license and registration, please?" said Highway Patrolman E. Dixon, after pulling the Infiniti over on the corner of Long Beach Blvd and Forhan.

"The reason I'm pulling you over, Mr. Grant," which was C Mac's last name, "was because you have a shattered backlight," said Patrolman Dixon, not knowing that this Infiniti was involved in a Wild Wild West shootout earlier.

Mitch sat there in the passenger seat and played it cool, as usual. He also had the 50cal in his waistband that was undetectable.

"I can smell a heavy odor of marijuana coming from your vehicle, sir," Patrolman Dixon said.

"Yeah… well, sir, we're just coming back from a party down there at Dominguez College, sir. We just finished the last of the blunt."

"No problem, man, we was all young once in our lives, so sit tight and let me run your info. If everything comes back good, y'all will be free to go," said Patrolman Dixon who looked like a rookie to the force.

Ten minutes later, everything seemed to check out good. Patrolman Dixon then wrote C Mac a fix it ticket.

"Have a nice evening," he hopped back on his patrol motorcycle and rode on to stop the next car passing car by so he can make his quota in tickets.

"Shit, nigga, that was damn near a close one," C Mac said, wiping the sweat from his forehead with his wife beater. He tossed his fix-it ticket out the window as he started his engine and pulled off.

"On my mama, things could have went bad real, quickly."

As Mitch saw his homie Julian at the store called London Market, he told him to gather all the TG's and tell them it was a meeting at Mitch's crib in a hour…

5:30 pm

At Mitch's crib were all the TG's, which numbered around twenty strong soldiers, were gathered in his backyard. They were barbecuing, smoking tree's, and drinking Avion Tiquila while some indulged in cocaine. Soon as the music that was playing the song "Beach City" by the group Long Beach Movement, which was put together by Long Beach's own Snoop Dogg, who put the LBC on the map. They had collectively gathered the tightest rapper from every hood in Long Beach and made them into the group Long Beach Movement.

"I gathered y'all here for this meeting because, not only for the new homies that just got recently put on and the fact I have some new toys for yall from the money y'all all pitched in with to cop," meaning the weapons. "Yall just be on point for anything," Mitch gave them the heads up about the Denver Lane Bloods. "They are going to slide through any day when they find out who killed their main, Shotcaller Bixyduece."

Mitch looked at life like the game of chess. He was very smart, sometimes too smart for his own good. He always was two steps ahead of everyone else.

"Just be on point and don't get caught slipping. That means, no more hanging out in front of the store. Everyone watch everyone's back," C Mac added.

"Do anyone have any questions or concerns?' Mitch asked.

Nobody had any questions.

As all the TG's left, shortly one after another, with their new guns and ammunition, they headed to hop in traffic. Some left to do their own thing, going back to the trap houses.

"I'll fuck with you in a minute, murda. I'm going to fuck with Tyanna from earlier. I already told her I was coming through," said C Mac. "What you bout to do?"

"Shit, I gotta go get my son from his grandmother's tonight," responded Mitch.

"Yep, I'll get with you. I'm about to hop in the wind tips, murda, tops," C Mac said as he walked back into his crib.

It was around 7:30 in the evening when Mitch got that phone call from Roddy. He was in the front, sitting in his van, smoking a wood, and sipping clear Tequila. He told Mitch he was waiting on him to hit the med shop. Roddy had multiple luxury cars, but his minivan was his lowkey car that he drove most of the time.

"What up, homie? Ride with me to the medical shop over there in the 50's," which was located off of 52nd and Atlantic, known as the Carmelito Projects.

"No doubt," Mitch agreed upon knowing that his son was under Amber's supervision.

Roddy was switching lanes through traffic while YG's song Just Want a Benz was bumping through the van's speakers when they pulled up.

Mitch hopped out to head inside the medical dispensary. The dispensary was in the gang territory Brick Boyz Crips. The Brick Boyz were once their rivals about fifteen years ago. However, that never really mattered to the Squarehood Hood Crips because they were well recognized, respected, and hated in the same token, everywhere on the North Side. Luckily, to Mitch's advantage, there was no one hanging out, not a soul, due to their current war with the 2NN Crips. They came through with multiple drive-bys everyday that week, taking out multiple of their front line soldiers.

On the ride back to the hood, they stopped at the park to blow their grams and watch the younger homie's conduct their business and patrol the turf. Mitch sat back and reclined his passenger seat. He twisted up a dutchee and pulled heavy on the indica weed. The two of them sat there overlooking one of his TG homies that go by the name Little Monster. They watched him make sale after sale until he ran out of all the work. He had it busted down into nickels, dimes, dubs, 50 double ups, and so forth, that he bought from Mitch a day ago. Big Monster was Little Monster's big brother from the set. He was murdered by a rival Mexican gang from Compton four years ago. He was shot in front of his apartment complex on the Westside of Long Beach.

As Mitch and Roddy sat there high and dazed, and lost in space, Mitch's cellphone broke the dead silence. It caught his attention when he seen his cell phone going off with the name C Mac on the caller ID. When Mitch answered, he sensed the urgency in C Mac's tone.

"What's up, loco?" Mitch asked.

"Just killed that bitch ass nigga, man," he was frantic. "I had to put some hot shells in em," replied a trigger happy C Mac.

He low key got a thrill out of killing. He looked at life as kill or be killed since being shot multiple times in his life. He was the 50 Cent of the hood.

"Who you talking about?" Mitch was confused.

"That bitch ass informant nigga Junebug!" he shouted.

"Yeah? Meet me at the crib. We can't discuss this over the phone."

"Yep, on my way now."

When C Mac pulled up to Mitch's crib, he hopped out frantically.

"I gave that snitch ass nigga Junebug slugs to the dome and all that."

"That nigga was the one who snitched on us to Deputy Thurman," C Mac said.

"Yeah? How you know that?" Mitch asked.

"Remember my hotline bling Tyanna that I said I was going to see?"

"Yeah," said Mitch.

"Well, remember that nigga Junebug's bitch that we seen at the mall?"

"Yeah, you talking about Rina."

"Yeah, she is homegirls with Tyanna. she told Tyanna and you know she told me everything."

"She told me that Junebug was the one who ratted on you about recently buying a half. And, he supposedly paid some young niggas from Bricc Boys named Big 50 Blue and his Goon Squad to come kill you out of hatred and for the success you have."

"Cuz bitch also stayed in the same apartment complex as mine, called the Springdales on the West Side," C Mac added. "So, when I heard that, I caught him in the underground parking lot structure and milked his bitch ass," C Mac said with a smirk on his face. "You know my motto, shoot first ask last," He pulled heavy on the backwood that was between his teeth.

"Cuz, we're drawing too much heat to the hood," Mitch said. He knew that they would have to lay extremely low because it was going to be a great deal of police patrolling the hood. He knew that if any murder happened in Long Beach, that was gang related, the LBPD assumed that the members of Squarehood had something to do with.

"Aye cuz, I'm thinking about enrolling into Compton College and get my AA. I want transfer to Long Beach State or something. I want to earn my degree in Creative Writing with my minor in African American History. You should enroll with me so we can get out the way and stay low," Mitch said.

"Yeah, you right," C Mac replied. "Who knows, maybe I can finally finish my certification for Auto Mechanics," C Mac said. Money, cars, clothes, and hoes was all that C Mac truly cared about, other than crippen and the murder game. He knew anything and everything there was to know about when it came to cars. "Yep, fuck it. I'm going to pick you up in the morning so we can go enroll into Compton College," C Mac said.

October 24th, 2013

8:15 am

Early in working the morning after Amber already left to drop their son, Nasir, who was at the tender learning age of 4, at his grandmother's house, and then headed off for work. Mitch had already been up since 4 o'clock. He was on his debut Urban Fiction novel. He was suddenly interrupted by his Galaxy Note 5 going off. It was C Mac. He stated that he was in front of his crib waiting with their homie Julian. He also wanted to enroll.

"I'ght here I come, murda, tips," Mitch replied.

As they drove through the college parking lot, they noticed all the hot young ladies walking around campus with books and backpacks. It reminded Mitch of why he loved to learn and attend school in the first place. The trio had a thrill seeing all the short dresses and tight jeans that hugged every inch of their body frames while walking around campus. All C Mac thought about when driving through the parking lot was seeing all these attractive smart girls was who was going to be his sixth babymomma.

"Cuz, is bitches all that you think about?" Mitch jokingly said with his signature cracked smile.

"Yup, sure do, murda," C Mac replied.

All three homies laughed together in unison.

Mitch didn't have no brothers, he only had sisters. Therefore, C Mac and Julian were more than homies to Mitch. They were like brothers. They all grew up together and did everything as one. They bust their first gun together, got put on together, and had their first piece of ass together.

Mitch's father, who didn't gang bang, was well respected in the hood but had such a terrible drinking problem. He was comrades with C Mac pops, as well with Julian's dad. Big C Mac, who had been locked up since the late seventies with an L for a triple homicide, he was doing his time in Corcoran Penitentiary. Julian's pops Big Yak, who was killed in a drive by shooting in 1996, always felt since his pops died by the gun that was his only destiny was to also die by the gun. Enrolling into college was something these three Crips always talked about since they were kids on the school playgrounds.

They all met up at the food court after meeting with their counselors and getting their schedules. Things were going smooth, they thought this was what Mitch had wanted for him and his homies.

"Shit, we start class tomorrow morning," Julian said. He was taking science the following morning. "What classes are you taking, homie?" Julian asked.

"Shit, I'm taking Automotive," C Mac replied.

Mitch chimed in, "I got English 108."

C Mac and Mitch were dropped Julian off at his crib. Daps and hugs were exchanged, not knowing that this was going to be their last time seeing their homie Julian. He was gunned down that night at the liquor store, by the hands of 50 Blue from Brick Boyz Crip.

May 1st, 2013

It was the last day of the semester. C Mac and Mitch was passing all their classes, staying out the way, and being undetectable. The hurt still lingered from the news they received about their homie Julian that was murdered seven months ago. No one knew who was the shooter. No one was charged with their homies demise. Julian's funeral was the talk of the streets for the last couple of months. They knew that revenge was a must once they found who to blame.

Mitch's english professor was a lady of great statue. She was and ex-panther and African American Activist who protested with Huey P. Newton, the name of Mrs. Bassett. She took a liking to Mitch through his writing and short stories because she knew it was detailing his own life. She seen that he was special and had a gift, she but knew he was deeply involved still in the streets.

"You have some talent, Mr. Matthew's," Mitch's professer said. "Why don't u send these in to some publisher's?" she asked.

"I never thought about that," Mitch replied.

"You know, I have a friend that's a publisher out here in Los Angeles, by the name of Terry L. Wroten. I spoke highly about you to him, some months back. I can read through you." Mrs. Bassett knew he was a bright individual who just needed some form of guidance. "Your writings tell a story. I can tell that you're living this life. I see that your writing is your way out."

What Mrs Bassett was explaining to Mitch was hitting home with each word she spoke.

"You have major talent, son. Your stories remind me of the great Paul Laurence Dunbar and Donald Goines," she explained to him with sincerity in her golden brown aged eyes.

"Yeah… thank you. I'll think about all your advice you've given," Mitch said to Mrs Bassett. He stood to leave class.

After school, Mitch linked up with C Mac, he was in his new ride. C Mac had bought a Dodge Challenger, sittin on 26's, in the schools parking structure.

"Tips, murda," was the lingo that Crips used daily when they greeted each other.

"Awe, cuz, I got some info to inform you about," said C Mac.

"Waddup, Crip?"

"I found out the nigga who killed the homie Julian," C Mac said with a firm look on his face. This was serious news for the both of them.

"Well, who did that shit, nigga?" Mitch said. He now had revenge on his mind. He leaned against the Challenger.

"That young ass nigga 50 Blue from the projects. The FEDS did gang sweeps and probation violation sweeps on documented gang members all over the city."

"Shit, what's cracking for Shante birthday?" Shante was there homegirl.

"I don't know, but she wanted to get her some tables at the Playhouse Club," Mitch said.

"Bet, I'm going to call the my nigga Tim, he works at the club and reserve us four tables," said C Mac.

C Mac was a Los Angeles County hood celebrity. He was known in every city and and every hood. A fat light skinned nigga with green eyes that was an advantage and disadvantage at the same time.

Later that night, Mitch took his whole family out to eat at the restaurant Sizzler, which was down the Blvd on Del Amo Street. Mitch wanted to get his family together to tell them his good news that he has been holding from them. He wanted to wait until he felt it was the right time to announce that the well known west coast author and publisher

Terry L. Wroten had agreed to review his portfolio and consider signing him to his No Brakes Publishing Company.

"I'm so proud of you, my sweet baby boy, and everything you're achieving that you set out for," said Mitch's mother, Mrs. Flossie.

Mrs. Flossie was also in attendance with Mitch's pops Mr. Matthew's, his baby mother Amber, his son Nasir, and his two sisters Jasmine and Monique. They all were happy for him, considering the lifestyle that he lived.

"My only baby boy, my son. I've always believed in you ever since you was young. I remember you running around the block with a Donald Goines book that you stole from my library, and that composition book that you always kept your short stories in. I knew you were destined for greatness," she said as she gave him hugs and kisses like he was twelve years old again.

After eating a big, five course meal, they were all stuffed and full. Mitch paid the bill and left a twenty dollar tip to the young female waitress that had served him and his family.

May 3rd, 2013

It was a day before their homegirl Shante's birthday. Mitch and C Mac, along with several other TG homies, accompanied with about seven young homegirls that claimed the same hood, was all kicking it at their big homegirl house, Patrice. She was the head female in charge of the hood. Everyone met at her house, which was off of Trafford and Long Beach Blvd. Patrice's crib was one of the many hood houses that the neighborhood shared.

The sounds of Ty Dolla Sign "Blase" was what filled the ongoing kickback. Everybody indulged in some drinking and smoking. A few homies hit the side of the house to snort some lines of cocaine. That was the TG's main hustle and main money maker, beside pushing ounces of Promethazine.

The TG's had about six cocaine houses within the hood to push from if they wasn't on the curb slanging. They had two Promethazine houses and one meth house where they was killing sales. They were making a fortune from slangin packs all day all night.

Mitch's organization was estimated to be somewhere around 800 thousand dollars. Mitch controlled all the drug trade due too being so close to Compton and near all the freeways that they trafficked their drugs from city to city, state to state.

Mitch was more than straight when it came to bankrolls. Mitch never left the house with anything under five stacks in his back pocket. Mitch was always low key and tried to keep a low profile. Unlike the rest of his homies. They loved to flash money, jewels, and their new hot rides.

The kickback was in full swing when one of the little TG's by the name of Young Jay mentioned

he was heading to the store with one of the
homegirls named Denise.

Denise and the rest of her crew were the
hoodrats of the North. They were down for watever,
but acted upscale for no apparent reason but to feel
like they were better than what they apparently
were.

"You strapped?" asked Mitch. "Since yall
bailing instead of driving."

"Yeah, I'm strapped," said Young Jay. He
lifted up his shirt, showing his blammer, which was
a .357. It was secured under his Gucci belt buckle.

"We gonna get another bottle and some food
from Louisiana Chicken," said Young Jay with
Denise following closely behind.

"Yep," another TG said.

As Young Jay and Denise were walking
back towards Patrice's house, they were
immediately stopped by the 12's. they lit them up
and swooped up on them. They hopped out four
deep like crazed madmen in the store parking lot.

"On the hood, off my squad car,"Deputy Boxer said.

Young Jay was sporting his every bit of blue and gold and bomber jacket with his Robbin jeans, accompanying his Jordan 10's to match. Denise was wearing her blue and gold spaghetti strap shirt with her white tight pants, hugging every curve of her stallion built physique. Square Hood Crips was written all over their faces.

"What the fuck y'all pigs got me bumped up for? I ain't doing shit nor have shit on me." He already stashed his heat in the store between the chips on the shelf.

Young Jay had already previously seen the 12's riding around and looking janky. They were waiting for them to come out to be jacked. Young Jay seen all this going on while Denise was up at the register paying for the alcohol and blunts.

Jay was on the hood of the squad car and Denise standing in the background with her arms folded.

"I'm just gonna run your punk ass homeboy name and make sure he's not wanted or being investigated for any murders that happened lately."

"Go ahead, shit. My name is good," Young Jay said. He was getting restless and fatigued from being on the hood of the squad car. The engine was still running and the heat from the hood was causing Young Jay hands to slowly burn and cause blisters and sores.

"Where's ya boy's, C Mac and Mitch? Yall know them?" asked Lieutenant Thurman.

"Nah, I don't even know who those niggas are. Never heard of em," shot back Young Jay.

The deputies knew he was lying.

"Well, get y'all black ass in the house and stay there because next time we come through here and see you, we're booking and taking your ass straight to jail. Now, get the fuck out of here!" Deputy Boxer yelled. "These are my streets!"

As soon as Young Jay and Denise made it back to Patrice's crib, Jay immediately went and informed Mitch and C Mac about their encounter with the Hit Squad.

"Yeah, they said all that?" Good lookin out, homie. Go ahead a make yall selves a drink," C Mac said.

Mitch heard the whole conversation. He sat there silent. He was in deep thought.

"Damn, you think they know it was us?" said, a now panicking C Mac.

"Nah, stay cool," Mitch said. Mitch was always was cool, calm, and collective at all tim

May 4th, 2013

Shante's party was in full swing at the hottest club in Hollywood, called Playhouse. Mitch, C Mac, Shante, Patrice, Tristan, Roddy and majority of the TG's and older homies, were all in attendance, taking up half of the club space. Anybody who was a somebody was at her birthday bash. From hustlers to pimps to reputable gang members of both sides of the flag, even local celebrities were present .There they were, partying the night away, and having a ball.

C Mac went as far as to have OT Genasis and Vince Staples rock the crowd with their smash hit single "Touchdown and Nate."

Mitch was in the back of the crowd, sipping Rose Moet and lifting his bottle towards Shante as they stood on stage. C Mac always had to be the center of attention on stage with the microphone in hand as he announced a happy C-day to the lovely Shante who just turned 21. Shante's Birthday Bash was one for the books.

Killa Twan was the only surviving Blood that made it out the car accident and deaths out of all three of his homies, in which was the shotcaller Bixyduece from Denver Lanes Bloods. Killa Twan was in the back of the club plotting his revenge on Mitch and C Mac. Killa Twan did his street homework to find out the location of where they were at. To his surprise, Killa Twan and his only two young soldiers, that he brought, were greatly outnumbered by fifty to their three.

Killa Twan and his foot soldiers managed to sneak their pistols into the club undetected.

The club was in full swing. C Mac was on stage drunk as a muthafucka. He grabbed the microphone from the host and put his bottle of champagne in the air. "This is for Long Beach, toast!"

Performing the last song of the night was Joe Moses. He performed his song Fresh Out as all the females ran to the center of the dancefloor to get their last dance in.

As the club began to let out, Killa Twan watched from a far. Mitch and C Mac stumbled out, whistling for a cab. They were with Amber and some random fine Puerto Rican girl that C Mac managed to snatch on the dance floor before the club let out.

"Fuck it, let's follow them to where they're going and then we're going to send them crab bitches straight to hell," Killa Twan said. He had been seeking revengeance for the last year for the death of Bixyduece.

Before both couples, for the night, hopped into two separate taxi cabs, one of the recent newly recruits, Terone, seemed to smuggle in the cab with C Mac and the Puerto Rican female.

"What the fuck, cuz! Nigga, why didn't you ride back to the hood with Patrice?" C Mac said, expressing his agitation.

"Cuz, that bitch drunk than a muthafucka. She knocked back two 5ths of pineapple Ciroc alone. Just drop me off at the hood store London's," Terone said as he sat closely to C Mac's date.

Both taxi cabs took off, heading towards the freeway on ramp. Following closely, in pursuit, was Killa Twan and his soldiers. They were driving a 2004 grey Lexus on 22-inch rims.

"Damn, Blood, where they heading to? Shit, we're already on the 91 freeway, heading east."

Little did they know, they were driving straight to the territory of Squarehood Crips.

"Well, shit, they getting off now. Keep a three dar distance in between us and y'all niggas load up," said Killa Twan, who was checking the magazine to his uzi that had plenty of murders on its belt. The other two Bloods were armed with two sawed off shot guns.

The taxi cab that shuttled C Mac and the Puerto Rican female, and Terone, pulled into London's Liquor Store. Amber and Mitch kept going straight, headed to their crib.

"Pull into this alleyway that's leading to the store front and hit your headlights so I can send them crab niggas to meet the reaper," said Killa Twan, in a bold tone.

When they pulled up, there were no homies hanging out in the set at this hour. No dice games cracking, no one striking up on the walls , nothing but death was in the air. Soon as Terone was exiting the cab at the store, he have daps to C Mac and within that same split second, all you heard were *fuck crabs!* trailing a hail of bullets from Killa Twan's Uzi and the heavy blasts from the two young Bloods shot guns.

Terone was hit with ten slugs, ripping through his chest, and spinning him in a full 360 spin. He was then greeted with a fatal shot from one of the young Blood's rounds that tossed him eight feet away. The puerto rican lady was caught in the crossfire, suffering one shot to the head, leaving her lifeless before her body even touch the ground. C Mac was shot in the shoulder while covering inside the taxi cab by one of the endless bullets from Killa's Uzi but somehow managed to escape by ducking low in the taxi as it sped off, leaving Terone and the Puerto Rican girl who's name was lizzy, head splattered all over the concrete.

Killa Twan and the young Bloods hopped back into traffic and managed to escape on the 110 freeway, heading North.

London's Liquor Store was now a warzone. Bodies filled the parking lot as all the nearby residents came running to see who was killed after that deadly shootout.

"We did it!" shouted the young Blood who was driving them back to their turfs with smiles on their face, knowing that they had someone's mother crying over their dead son.

The Channel 2 News reporters were at the bloody murder scene with their microphones and cameras, just after Gang Task Force Deputity Boxer and Thurman taped off the scene. On every corner, the Sheriff's blocked and directed oncoming traffic.

Dee Dee, along with the other TG homies Little Devil, Baby Spank, Baby Tone, and other's, were allfilled with anger as they were trying to make their way to the front of the store to see their homie laid out, riddled from bullets.

Two weeks later, was Tyrone's funeral. All the TG's were in attendance along with their OG's who also paid their last respects to their little homie. The local police was out front standing guard in front of Ebenezer Baptist Church that was located on Artesia and Butler that was two miles from there hood. The church was flooded with their gang colors and weeping females. Dee Dee was there trying to hold back his tears while seeing his cousin laying in that closed casket. All that was running through his mind was death upon those that took a piece of his family away.

As the church was being let out, all the gang members got in their cars and followed the hearse up Artesia to Cherry Street where the graveyard was located. They sat and watched them put their homie into the ground six feet deep.

Before the maintenance men started shoveling dirt, Mitch, C Mac, Baby Spoke, and Little Devil each threw blue bandannas onto his casket as it was being lowered into the dirt.

"We love you, homie. 4 in peace," they all said at the same time.

"Gone but never forgotten. We Crips, we dont die, we multiply," said C Mac as everyone who came to pay their respects said their final goodbyes.

Back at Mitch's crib, after the repast, they held a secret meeting amongst all the TG's.

"It was some Bloods that took our Loc," saying the second in command c mac.

"I seen his face and it was that slob nigga Killa Twan who killed Terone. We was in the county jail together, cuz from Denver Lanes said C Mac. "This means war," C Mac also added.

Everyone else in attendance of the meeting agreed.

"So, what about them Bricc Boy niggas who been striking up on the outside skirts of the hood walls?" asked a young tg by the name of tank.

"You know they never liked us, anyway, since their homie got robbed by the big homies in the dice game at the park," added another trigger happy homie named no good.

"Fuck them niggas, they ain't popped shit yet. They ain't trippin," said a blindly Mitch, who didn't believe that, before junebug died. He put money on his head.

June 5th, 2014

"So, what University do you plan on going to, babe? You just received your AA degree and I'm very proud of you and the progress you're making by going back to school and receiving a degree," said amber.

"Thank you, love, and I'm not sure yet. I'm still undecided and debating if I wanna go to Long Beach State or take, y'all, my family out of state for college and go to an HBCU," replied Mitch as they were sitting at the table as a family while eating dinner.

"I mean it's up to you, baby. I'm here to support you all the way in whatever decision you make," amber said.

As Mitch was washing the dishes while amber was tucking their son nasir in for bed, he was in deep thought about determining what University to attend. The talks he had with his professor suggesting that Mitch should attend Howard University, located in Washington DC, to earn his Bachelor's Degree in Creative Writing and Communications. She suggested a school up north that was practically an all historical black college. she knew the kind of lifestyle that Mitch was living behind her classroom walls. She knew that it would be a great and new opportunity for him and his family. Mitch was stuck on staying home and making a difference by slowing down and eventually hang up his flag. He wanted to show the younger generation that there's always another way to do things. It's something that Mitch had to ponder on for a awhile.

Mitch was done washing the dishes. He entered their master bedroom and laid in bed. Mitch and Amber started eating a bowl of popcorn while sipping on some moscato wine and watching the Tyler Perry movie Madea. As they were watching the movie, things started to heat up. After three bottles of Moscato, hormones started to flare. Mitch started to kiss on Amber's neck while nibbling on her ear. Not long after they were soon in the 69 position. Mitch was flicking his tongue, hitting every G spot that was sending exotic chills up her legs. He turned her over on her back and slid in every inch of his manhood.

"Who's daddy?"

"You are, yes, you are, daddy," Amber said as she enjoyed every bit of the pounding.

"Whose pussy is this?" Mitch groaned in excitement.

"This is yo pussy, daddy. You gonna give me another baby, I'm cumming, daddy!" Amber let go of all her Goddess fluids. That made Mitch even more aroused as he kept going deeper and slower.

Not soon after, Mitch's legs started tingling. He couldn't hold on any longer, he nutted all inside of his baby mother. They lay there in silence, holding each other for comfort until amber dozed off to sleep.

Mitch slipped from under her grasp to run a shower. After his shower, he went into his office, rolled up some dutchee's, and reflected on all the events that had been happening the last two year's, good and bad. From all the funerals he had attended to the ongoing gang war that had been sweeping his very own streets. He looked above on the wall and looked at his son's picture. He then realized all that he had done was well worth it. He then cracked open his laptop.

June 6th, 2014

9:38 Am

"Yo, murda, come ride with me to go collect our money from the trap spot that the TG homie Tank is running and then let's hit Roscoe's for some breakfast."

"I'ght… no doubt, pick me up from the barber shop. I'm on Atlantic, I'm a just leave my whip," replied Mitch.

"Yo, Mitch, that nigga c mac pullin up."

"I'ght, good looking, cuz," said Mitch. He slid his barber twenty five dollars in his hand. He then dusted his shoulder. Mitch's Desert Eagle was seen in clear view, sitting on his hip.

Mitch exited the barber shop and hopped into C Mac's ride. He was bumping that new Joey Fatts I'll Street Blues album.

"Yo, how much we collecting?" asked Mitch. He already knew, but wanted to see if c mac kept up with the count or was he skimming from off top, which he knew he was.

"Yeah, Loc, it's twelve thousand six a piece, nigga, I know."

"Nah, nigga. See where the fuck you went to school at, cuz, definitely not to Jordan because you don't know your math," Mitch joked.

"Cuz, it's thirteen thousand. Seven thousand for me and six for you, cuz," Mitch responded.

"Aye cuz, fuck you. I was seeing if you remember, nigga," C Mac said as he started to pull off.

"Yeah, since we're here, I'm a twist up while you call that nigga and tell em we're outside, Mitch said as he twisted up a Dutch Master.

"Yo, cuz, we outside."

Alright, fosho. I'm coming out now," Tank replied.

"So, where do you see yourself in the next five years?" Mitch asked out of the blue.

"Shit, honestly still fucking these bitches, still getting this money, and still hanging and banging. Why yous ask, nigga?" C Mac asked, curious to what Mitch was getting at.

"Shit, nigga, we bout… well, let me rephrase, I'm thinking about enrolling into an HBCU primarily Howard University. Man, I'm thinking about enrolling and taking my family out there while I get this last bit of education so a young Crip can graduate and really do something."

"Cuz, you don't need no fucking piecee of paper from a school to validate your success, Loc. You done did it all that a gangsta could possibly do, Crip. Especially now that you're trying to do your shit with this book shit you got cracking. See me, I just did Junior College simply for the hoes. You know bitches all try and say they want an education or some sort, that's why I went. I'm still impressed at myself that I stayed that long to receive my AA," C Mac responded.

"Here Tank Loc comes now," C Mac said.

"What up, Crips?" Tank threw a brown paper bag filled with the thirteen thousand, all big face hundreds and fifties, onto Mitch's lap.

"How's it's looking?" asked Mitch giving him dap.

"Shit, lovely, my shift bout to be over in a hour. What yall niggas about to get into? I know y'all about to go eat and stuff y'all faces."

"Yeah, and you know it," said c mac with his grin that was holding the Dutchee in his dental.

"Nah, we bout to hit Roscoe's, wanna roll, crip?" Mitch asked.

"Nah, y'all can go ahead, I'll catch up with y'all in a few. I'm bout to go meet up with this little hottie I met at the Lakewood Mall, in a minute. yYall good, though?" Tank asked.

"Yep, we always good, murda," C Mac pulled his two twin glocks from under his seat.

"Yeah, I hear talk in the streets that them niggas from Brick Boys is tryna start something."

"Man, fuck them niggas. Them niggas ain't talkin bout shit, they ain't making no noise," C Mac shot back.

"Yeah, you right," Tank laughed off C Mac's pumped attitude as he headed back into the spot.

"Shit, Roscoe's it is!"

C Mac pulled off and turned up the the music that was subbing from his car.

"What you ordering toda,y Loc? The usual Obama special?" asked c mac in a jokingly manner.

"Yeap, you already know, and you got jokes today, huh, cuz?" shot back Mitch with his smirk on his face.

"So, what we get for you two gentlemen?" the middle aged waitress asked.

"Yeah, we would like to order now. Can we have the Obama special with a Coca-Cola along with some chicken wings and fries with a Sprite as well," C Mac said.

"No problem. Your food should be done and brought out within 15 to 20 minutes," said the middle-aged waitress.

"So, what you gonna do with your money, cuz? I hope you invest it into something legit, loc," Mitch said.

Before c mac was going to answer, Mitch's cell phone began to ring.

"Yeah, wassup?" Mitch answered.

"Yo, I need four of them thangs. I'm at the spot on Artesia and Poppy, sitting out front in the car," said Scrap Loco, a young soldier and hustler from 2NN Crip.

Scrap Loc and Mitch go way back, all the way back to elementary when they used to be chasing the girls and hustling lunch tickets.

"Alright, no doubt. Give me about 30 minutes," said Mitch.

"Alright, bet," Scrap Loc responded.

"Yo, cuz, we gotta take this food to go. I gotta meet up with Scrap, he's tryna cop," Mitch said as he stood from the table.

"No doubt, homie. Let me just tell her to change our orders to to-go, and then imma drop you off at yo car," C Mac said.

After Mitch got dropped off to his car, Mitch drove to one of his spots to put together Scrap's package. Here he was, in the kitchen putting together four and a baby, scaling everything up in accordance.

"Yo, Scrap Loc, I'm on my way over now. I'll be there in about ten minutes. I'm hoppin in my car now."

"No doubt," replied Scrap Loc.

Mitch walked into his garage to stash the four and a baby in his car, he hopped in, turned on the stereo that was playing 56 Nights by Future as he pulled out from his garage and headed East down Artesia.

"Yo, I'm pulling up now."

"I'ght fosho… I'm still sitting in the car, crip," Scrap Loc said.

"What's cracking with you, big dog?" Mitch tossed the package into Scrap's lap, giving him dap.

"Good looking and what's the deal?" asked scrap as he put the package under the seat.

"Shit, nothing really just coming from Roscoe's Chicken and Waffles with C Mac," Mitch responded.

"Right, right… wanna go in the crib and have a drink of Hennessy," Scrap asked.

"No doubt, homie."

The both of them exited Scrap's car.

-

Hitting the corner in their unmarked car was Hit Squad's Lieutenant Thurman and his deranged partner, Deputy Boxer.

"On the hood, the both of you. This is a shakedown!" Deputy Boxer lashed out to the both of the young Crips.

"What the fuck yall jacking us up for?" spat Scrap Loc. Luckily, he left the dope in his car. He had it under the seat and locked so it went unnoticed by the police officer's.

"Do you have any guns, drugs or weapons that can hurt me or my partner?" asked Deputy Boxer as he searched and patted down both men. They had their hands on top of their head, standing in front of their squad car.

"Nah, we ain't got shit. I'm just chopping it up with my cousin. He came to visit me," Scrap Loc said in a agitated tone.

"Hell, did you find anything?" asked Lieutenant Thurman as he sat in the squad car on the radio. He was talking to a dispatcher, running Scrap Loc identification whicj came back clean.

"Nothing found, sir," replied Deputy Boxer. Now, he was angry.

"You know what, Mitch? take a good look at my face because this the last face you are going to see after I bring you, your friends, and your organization down," said Lieutenant Thurman as he walked over to the silent Mitch. "Just a matter of time before I get all you bastards off my streets for good. Just a matter of time," he spat.

"Yeah, you think so?" Mitch clapped back with his devious smile. "You black niggers think y'all so tough with y'all guns and reputation out here on these streets, huh?" Deputy Boxer through in.

"Y'all better off dead, in my eyes. Y'all helping us out, anyway, by killing one another and destroying y,all own community with this poison yall been feeding," Boxer added with laughter.

"Get the fuck outta here!" Lieutenant Thurman growled as they drove off on another gang related shooting call from dispatch.

"Man, them mothafucka's been sweating us all fucking morning. They're up to something sneaky," Scrap Loc said to Mitch.

"Shit yeah, you're right. Well, I'm about to bust a move. I'm a go pick up my son, go hit the

Lakewood Mall and grab my little nigga some shoes and clothes."

"Indeed, and how your little man doing, anyway?"

"Bet... he's bigger than me already," Scrap jokingly said.

"Yeah, he big and reckless. A busy body but that's my mini me. Well, let me bust a move," said Mitch. He gave daps to Scrap Loc before he walked off. He then got into his Audi and pulled off, headed back East down Artesia.

-

Mitch and his son Nasir hit majority of every store within the mall. They walked out with multiple bags from all of the designer stores. He bought Ralph Lauren, Carter's for kids, Gucci, and some Chanel for Amber. Mitch spent somewhere around the total of six grand.

As Mitch was getting into his car after buckling his son up in his chair, Mitch's cell phone began to ring with the name reading of Tristan, his big homie.

"What's cracking, loc?" What's it looking like?" asked Tristan.

"Shit, just now leaving the mall from doing a little shopping. What you got up?" Mitch responded. "Shit, the usual, posted watching Sports Center. Come through and bring some blunts, come watch the Lakers game," Tristan added.

"No doubt, I'ma come through after I drop my little man off at his grandmother's, and then I'm a be on my way. Scrap Loc from 2NN's is going to meet up with me at the store."

"Shit, the both of y'all can come through, it's no problem," Tristan insisted.

7:15 pm

"Aye, ma, come here,' Mitch said too a young Gina who was walking to the store with five of her attractive young homegirls who all ran together.

Mitch was sitting in his car watching traffic go by while twisting up some blunts when Gina seductively walked up to his passenger window.

"What's up, big homie?" she asked while licking her lips.

Gina was a little sister to Mitch, he always looked out for her since an early age. Gina knew Mitch didn't look at her like that but that didn't stop Bina from flirting with him.

"How's it's looking? What you and your homegirl's up to?" Mitch asked.

"Shit, nothing really, Mitch. we just getting a 5th of Remy Martin and some Backwoods. Then we're going back to my crib to play dominoes, cards, and order some pizza. You know you always welcome to come by, boo," Gina spoke in a soft and sexy tone.

"Yeah, that's wassup. I'm a probably swing by in a few with a couple of my homies, if that's cool," Mitch asked.

"Yeah, boo, like I said, you're always welcome at my house and you should bring your friends for my homegirl's," Gina said back.

"Okay, no doubt and you crazy, little homie," Mitch laughed.

Scrap Loc pulled up right on the side of Mitch in perfect timing so he could get a first hand look of all her homegir's that gathered behind her, gossiping.

7:27pm

"Ayo, wassup, loco? Where y'all at with it?"
Roddy spoke into the receiver.

"Shit, we right here at the little homegirl
crib on Harcourt. Come through, murda, she having
a kickback with some of her homegirl's," Mitch
said.

"Yep, no doubt. I'm getting off the 91
Freeway now," Roddy hung up and exited the
freeway.

10:30 pm

Not less than half a mile from getting off the freeway, Roddy seen the lights flashing through his rear view mirrors. He knew it was the Sheriff's, practically the Hit Squad, who tank swore to himself before he left the penitentiary that he wasn't going back.

"Well, look at what we have here," Deputy Boxer said.

"Wassup, officer's?" said Roddy. He was trying to not break a sweat, knowing he had about 100 grams of powder cocaine in his secret compartment in his ride.

Gina's homegirl, Brandice, went back up to the liquor store for some more Swishers and ice for the liquor, seen that Roddy stopped on the other side of the road by the Sheriff's. She started being nosey as she always did. She then called her homegirl Gina.

"Let me see your license and registration. Are you on probation or parole?" asked Deputy Boxer who already know Roddy was.

"Why do we gotta go through this every time?" Roddy asked. "Y'all already know I'm on parole and that I have license and registration. I'm legit," Roddy shot back, now getting agitated from the police who are always harassing young black males.

Roddy kept his cool, he knew he had 100 grams of cocaine is in the car and Deputy Boxer was known for bringing the K9 dog. He had one it numerous of times.

"What are you doing around here, anyway?" Lieutenant Thurman asked.

"Just visiting my little cousin," Roddy replied. "He has a basketball game in a hour, sir."

"Yeah fucking right," Boxer snapped.

Deputy Boxer was angry with Roddy and anybody accociated with him. He didn't like or respect Roddy. He hated that they were making large sums of money right under their nose.

"Get out of here and don't let me catch you again around here or I'm booking you on gang injection. This is your final warning," said the Lieutenant with fire in his tone.

"No problem," Roddy said with a smirk on his face, knowing that he dodged another close bullet.

-

Gina's kickback was in full swing. They were drinking and smoking loud while they enjoyed the sounds of Ty Dolla Sign that was blasting through the speakers. The hoodrats were gossiping as usual while all the TG's and local residents participated in the ongoing big money dice game outside on the patio.

"Cuz, I'm a hit this seven and take all you niggas money on the ground," said c mac, laughing with his wad of big bills in his hand.

"I got 100 he come out 7 or 11," Mitch threw in, tossing a crisp blue hundred under his black and white low top Chuck Taylor's.

"Bet," another young homie said, throwing his currency on the ground.

Roddy placed a 100 dollar side bet also while looking onto the game.

"Seven, bitch, give me all that money!" c mac yelled as he hit seven on the opening roll.

As the night was coming to an end, most of the young TG's went their separate ways, some of them found dates with some of gina's homegirl.

"What you bout to get into?" Roddy asked Mitch.

"Shit, I'm going to stay here for a minute and holla at Gina. What you bout to get into, murda?" Mitch asked while taking sips of the champagne he poured himself.

"Shit, really. About to go fuck with this bitch and go eat out there in Hollywood at the Standard."

"Fosho, cee safe, murda," as he's givin a dap to Roddy as he's leaving and hopping into his van starting up his engine.

"Pull the fuck over!" Deputy Boxer shouted through the speakercom.

"What the fuck did I do now?" Roddy said as he pulled over.

"Fuck, y'all just pulled me over no more than three hours ago, what the fuck y'all want with me, pigs?" Roddy turned down his stereo. He was playing Lil Boosie Fuck the Police.

"Get the fuck out the car!" Deputy Boxer opened Roddy's door with a quickness, causing Roddy's Beretta to slide and fall onto the pavement, right in front of the Sheriff's.

"Now look what we have here, you son of bitch," sneered Deputy Boxer.

"Fuck," Roddy mumbled under his breath, knowing he had to make a quick decision. He knew that they were going to search his car and find the dope.

Within a split second, before Boxer could reach for his gun, Roddy drew his chrome .38 and shot twice at the deputy boxer and lieutenant Thurman, causing them to duck for cover.

Pop pop! was what the deputies heard as Roddy tried to make a getaway on foot. He ran through the neighborhood, hopping fence to gate. He then hid in someone's back house that wasn't occupied at that time.

Within two minutes, the byrd (helicopter) was out in the sky hovering over the house that Roddy hid in.

"Shots fired, shots fired! Letinuant Thurman has been hit twice in the chest. We need medical ASAP!" Boxer helped his partner while he gasped for his last breath.

Deputy Boxer ripped open Thruman's uniform shirt to see where he was hit at. That's when he saw the two bullet holes that went through his bulletproof vest. Blood was flowing out his body at a rapid pace. He sat there and watched his partner turn pale while losing every breath he took.

By the time the ambulance arrived with the backup units of Sheriff's, it was already too late for letinuant Thurman, he had passed a couple of seconds upon their arrival.

"Imma kill all them son's of bitches!" Deputy Boxer said with fire and death in his eyes.

Roddy was captured two hours later after a gun battle standoff. He was sitting in the sub station waiting for the bus to take him back to the Los Angeles County Jail from the Lynwood Sheriff's Station. He was now facing murder on a police officer, attempted murder, and the 100 grams of cocaine that they found after searching his vehicle…

June 7th, 2014

9:30 am

"Yo! Mitch, answer your damn phone, Roddy in jail, man. Bang my line when you receive this message." Tritian had left Mitch several messages.

After a long night of drinking and smoking at Gina's kickback, Mitch was awaken by the sound of his Galaxy Note 5 ringing off the hook. After listening and seeing all his missed calls, Mitch turned down his stereo from the sounds of Nas banging Ether to dial Tristan's cell phone.

Ring ring ring.

"Yo, hello? What up, Mitch? Cuz, I know you already heard about Roddy."

"Yeah, I just heard about it not too long ago,"Mitch added. He was hurt about Roddy being locked up. He knew soon enough that his organization was going to have to now meet Roddy's connect, Rafel, in Lakewood.

"Damn, he in there for murder on a police officer, attempted murder, weapons, and drug possession charges."

"Do Rafel know about him being arrest yet?" Mitch asked.

"Nah, not yet that I know of..."

"Do he have a bail amount set yet?"

"Nah, not yet. He goes to court in two days so we will see what's up," Tristan added in a nonchanlant tone. He was concentrating on counting his stacks of money while talking on the phone.

"No doubt, call our lawyer Mr. Sanchez for Roddy and hit me after his first court appearance with the updates," Mitch said before hanging up his cell phone.

"Ight, bet," Tristan agreed to as he hung up his receiver on his end.

Mitch pulled out his cell phone and dialed c mac's number. C Mac finally answered on the fourth ring.

"Yo, what up, murda?" c mac said through the phone.

"Wanna go get some breakfast from Roscoe's and find out what we gonna do about Roddy's situation?" Mitch asked.

"Fasho, I haven't ate all morning, anyway," c mac replied.

"Alright, meet me at my crib and we can take my whip," Mitch said.

"Alright, fasho. I'm a be over there within the next 30 minutes, loco," c mac said as he hung up his cell phone.

10:37 am

"So, what would you two gentlemen like to order?" said the young jamaican waitress. Her hips were so wide, they could paint an iceberg sculpture the way she swayed back and fourth, heading to their table. "Can I start you guys off with a cup of coffee or maybe a cola?"

"Yeah that sounds nice. Can I have the coffee with that Obama Special with some grits," Mitch said as he gave the young waitress his menu.

"And for you, sir," she looked over and asked c mac. He was already undressing her as she was speaking to Mitch.

"Yeah, can you bring me an omelette and a breakfast burrito with a Sprite, beautiful" C Mac gave the young waitress a sexual look while handing back her his menu.

"Aye, cuz, you have always been a fool with the ladies ever since we was kids," Mitch said as he was trying to contain his crooked smile following after with laughter.

"Yeah, I know it was just something about pussy that drove me crazy, cuz," c mac said while breaking out in a hysterical laugh.

"Watch, I'm going to crack her," c mac said confidently with nothing more than lust in his eyes.

"You a fool," Mitch laughed laughed. He then started to relax in the booth, thinking about his family.

"Here you two gentlemen go, be careful because the plates are still hot," the young Jamaican waitress said as she placed the tray of food on their table.

"Thanks, boo, for everything, you are truly a lifesaver," said c mac. He was trying to shoot game at the young waitress.

She turned to walk off with her wide smile that seem to have made her morning.

Before Mitch could even grab his knife and fork, his cell started to ring out loud. It was Rafael's name flashing across the top.

"Yo, it's that fool Rafel. How the fuck he get my direct number?" Mitch said in a confused tone. "Answer that muthafucka, it's the plug who been supplying Roddy and the hood," C Mac said with his hustler's ambition smile written all over his face.

"Yo, what's up, is this Mitch?" Rafel asked before getting down to business.

"what's the deal, this Mitch," he replied.

"Yo, Mitch, this is rafel. What happened to Roddy? I heard he got locked up last night. I seen that shit on the Channel 7 News all last night."

"What up, rafel? And yeah, shit went real sour for him but we holdin it down, though. He should be in contact with our lawyer as we speak," Mitch said.

"Did you speak to Roddy yet and what we gonna do about our business?" Rafel asked, he was puzzled about what was going to happen with business.

"Shit, naw, I haven't heard from him yet."

"Well, do you think you can meet up with me later on this week so I can talk to you?" rafael asked.

"No doubt, rafel, just tell me when and where, and then I'm a go holla at Roddy and see how he is holding up, and talk about our next moves so we can pick up from there."

"No problem. I'll give you a call within a couple of days and I'll give you further instructions from there," said rafel as he's hung up the receiver on his end.

"What that fool say?" C Mac asked.

"Shit, he heard about what happened to Roddy and asked for me to meet up with him sometime this week and talk about our future and supply," answered Mitch.

"So, does that mean we have Roddy's connect?" C Mac asked with a grin on his face. He was already adding up the money that would be soon rolling in since Mitch would be dealing with Rafael, the Lakewood connect, directly.

"I dont know, cuz," responded Mitch, "but we're gonna see."

Within that minute, Mitch's cell phone started going off again, this time it was a Texas number which Mitch knew it was the Los Angeles County Jail.

"Hello, yo, Mitch, Waddup?" Roddy said on the other end. He was standing in the substation waiting to head to the county jail.

"What's the word?" Mitch responded.

"Shit, mane, it's all bad for me. They have me for murder and attempted murder with drug trafficking charges, cuz," Roddy dropped his head in disgust.

"Yeah, they can't hold a real one down for too long, such as yourself. Did you call the lawyer Mr. Sanchez yet?" Mitch asked.

"Yeah, loco, I just got off the phone with him a couple of minutes ago. He said he is going to see me in a couple of days at the county jail."

"Fosho, I'ma come see you too with Mr. Sanchez. Keep yo head up and stay sucka free," Mitch said, talking to his big homie Roddy.

"No doubt, love one, stay safe out there on the street's from these bitch ass niggas and especially move carefully since the FEDS are on us, crip," Roddy said. That's when he heard the automatic recording say, *"you have one minute left for your call."*

"Shit, you ready, murda?" Mitch asked.

"Yeah, we can dip, but first let me grab another refill," C Mac said as he grabbed another refill and the two made their exit swiftly.

June 8th, 2014

7:45 AM

"Yo, you got that for me, murda?" Mitch asked.

"Yeah, I got that for you, homie, the whole thang," Tank said. He was working one of the crack houses.

"I'ght, bet. I'm a be around their to pick up in about 15 minutes," Mitch said as he was hanging up his cell phone.

"I'ght, no problem," Tank shot back.

Sitting in a beige colored Lexus with tinted windows at the south end of the block sat 50-Blue from Bricc Boys Crip with another young soldier Rico. Rico was always ready to put in work, spinning the barrel to his 38 revolver. 50-Blue wasn't the only ones scooping out Mitch's moves and hangouts. Sitting on the north end of the block sat a blue AT&T van. The was occupied by a couple of Federal Agents that were sitting inside of the van. They were taking pictures of the crack house and Mitch's BMW as he bent the corner and parked in front of the crack house.

"Yo, loco, I'm outside. Bring that out for me," said Mitch as he turned down his stereo that was bumping Joey Fatts song Million Dollar Dreams.

"I'ght, here I come now," Tank replied.

"What up, Crip?" It's all there," Tank said said as he tossed a brown paper bag filled with all drug money that totaled up to 10,000 dollars.

They gave each other daps.

"I don't have to count it, do I?" asked Mitch as he lit up his dutchee. He took a couple of pulls and passed it to Tank.

"Come on, cuz, have I ever came short?" Tank shot back at him, trying to hold his cough in from the strong weed that they were smoking.

Click click click

The agents in the van snapped and got all the pictures of the money transition between the two. The FEDS were trying to build a strong case against Mitch to send him away for life.

"Look, cuz, there that fool goes right there," rico said as he pointed in Mitch's direction when he saw Mitch and Tank sitting on his BMW chopping it up.

"You ready to ride?" 50-Blue said as he checked his clip.

"Hell yeah I'm ready, ready to get it cracking and make a name for myself out here," hot headed Rico said.

"Fuck it, lets go peel they caps back. 50-Blue and Rico made their way out the car and headed towards the two young Crips with their pistols pointed down to their sides.

"Yo, cuz, who are these fools walking up?" Tank said as he started to withdraw his 45.

Before Mitch could even turn around to see who was walking up on them, he was hit in the shoulder by 50-Blue's hot flame thrower, knocking him to the ground.

Boom Boom Boom!

A gun battle quickly erupted in the middle of the street in broad daylight. Tank fired back six shots, hitting Rico smack dead in the chest, throwing him a couple of feet back, leaving him gasping for air as blood fills up his lungs. Mitch recovered and withdrew his 44. Desert Eagle and started blasting at 50-Blue. He hit him with all eight rounds. The bullets ripped through his thigh, torso, and face. As the shootout was taking place, the FEDS snapped and recorded the gangster execution style murder while Mitch stood over 50-Blue. he reloaded his Desert Eagle and unloaded his whole clip into 50-Blue's lifeless body.

After the last round penetrated 50 blue's body, he hopped into his BMW, fired his engine, and jetted into traffic. Tank fled the scene and dumped his pistol into the sewer drain not too far away. He ran in the opposite direction before the police made their presence with sirens closing in.

"Damn, nigga, answer your phone," Mitch said to himself as he continued to dial C Mac's number while trying keep the blood from running down his shoulder.

"Hello, what's cracking?" C Mac said. He was high as a kite.

"Shit, nigga, where you at? I'm about to pull up on you. I gotta holla at you, Crip," Mitch said.

"Shit, everything good, loc? I'm at Tyanna's crib, pull up."

"Yep, I'll be there in the next fifteen minutes," Mitch said as he gunned down the highway to Tyanna's crib.

"Yo, I'm outside, murda," Mitch said.

"I'ght, I'm coming, nigga. You can stop blowing your horn," C Mac said as he grabbed his 9mm glock from off the nightstand and made his way towards the front door.

"Yo, cuz, everything good? I was just in there bout to smack Tyanna ass," C Mac said as he entered Mitch's BMW.

"I killed that mothafucking faggot 50 Blue and his homie," Mitch said as he wrapped his shirt around his shoulder. The bullet had went in and out of his back.

"I'm a gather some homies up and we're going to ride through their projects and lay everything down, I mean everything for them to even think that they can fuck with us Squarehood Crips," said a vengance C Mac with death in his voice.

"You good, though, cuz? It look like you might need to go to the hospital."

"Nah, I'm good it went in and out," replied a nonchalant Mitch as he tied his shirt around his shoulder to help stop the bleeding.

"Well, shit, the project niggas are going to have to feel nothing but hollow points," said c mac as he lit up a Newport that sat between his dentals.

June 11th, 2014

10:32 AM

"Aye yo, Mitch, can you meet me at my crib so we can discuss our future?" Rafel asked as he was sitting on his couch petting his pet cat.

"No doubt, homie. I'll be over shortly with my man Tristan," Mitch replied as he poured himself a glass of Avion Tequila.

About an hour later, Mitch and Tristan were on the freeway headed to meet Rafael, the connect in Lakewood.

"Yo, cuz, this were that nigga Roddy was coming to all along to get our supply," Tristan said as Mitch was driving through what seemed like a wealthy neighborhood.

Mitch then pulled his BMW into the driveway of Rafael's home.

"Let's go get this money," Mitch told Tristan as they both exchanged daps while exiting the car. They then walked up the walkway.

As Mitch and Tristan were about to ring the doorbell, they were greeted by a short old Puerto Rican by the name of Rafael. He stood at 4'11 in height but seemed very hipped to the young game.

"Come in, my friend's," Rafel opened the screen door for the two men. "Have a seat, please. Are any of you guys thirsty?" he asked.

"Nah, we're good, thanks for asking, though," Mitch said.

"Right, let's get right down to business because that's why you guys are here for, anyway, huh?" Rafael said as he sat on the couch. "So with Roddy being locked up, I contacted you, Mitch, because I've been hearing your name throughout the streets," Rafel said. "I wanna keep doing business with your organization and give you a lower price from what I was charging Roddy. The reason I am doing this is because the guy you killed the other day, 50 Blue from the projects. He was giving some of my workers problems. Because of that, you have eliminated a big problem in my business."

"How you know that was me?" asked a puzzled Mitch.

"Come on, baby, I'm rafel. I know everything that goes down on these streets," Rafel popped his collar.

"Damn," Mitch laughed and nodded his head.

"I want you as a partner in my business, I have major political connects with some law officials in my pocket. Besides, I hear the FEDS are on you as well by the name of Deputy Boxer, so you kinda need me more than I need you," Rafel opened a can of Corona beer.

"Shit, with prices like that I'll be stupid not to partner with you," Mitch had his mind made up.

"Okay, excellent. My man's will hit you in a couple of days with some product and then I'll call you with further instructions," Rafel stood up to show Mitch and Tristan to the front door.

"Do you think we can trust that old man like that, Mitch?" Tristan asked asked as they were getting into the BMW.

Mitch started his engine."Yeah, everything's gonna be gravy, especially with the prices he is talking. We're gonna sew up all of California, we won't have shit to worry about," Mitch said while lighting up a ducthee that was sitting in the car's ashtray.

"Yeah, you right," Tristan said, pushing any negative thoughts he had about their new supplier to the back of his mind.

Mitch was looking forward to the future while puffing on the dutchee that was passed to him from Tristan as they got ghost into the morning traffic.

June 11th, 2014

10:32 PM

"Damn, daddy, when can we just say fuck all this here in California and just pack up and go, baby, like you said," amber said to Mitch as she was laying on his chest watching Love and Hip Hop. "We got well enough money put up. You know these streets dont love no one out there. Majority of your friends are dying or getting locked up. I don't wanna ever see that happen to you, babe," Amber pleaded with sincerity in her eyes and a concerning tone. "Me and Nasir need you with us every night."

"Don't trip, babe, we're gonna go on a vacation real soon, ma," Mitch said while removing the hair that hung over amber's face that was lightly covering her eyes. "I'm thinking bout making a few more power moves, stacking up a couple more bands, and leaving this game alone for good," Mitch also stated. "I'm ready to take my writing to the next level, babe."

"Are you sure, baby? because some nights I have intense nightmares of you never coming back home to us, baby," amber said with tears now starting to fall from her eyes.

"Baby, don't ever worry about that. I promise I'm never going anywhere," Mitch wiped away her tears.

"Baby,I 'm saying all this to say that I'm pregnant again. I'm about 5 weeks" Amber said.

"Yeah, is that right?" Mitch asked with a halh of a smile on his face.

"Yeah, baby, that's why im so ready to leave this horrible place and start a better life somewhere else, you know?"

"Yeah, I know… don't worry, baby, I got us," Mitch said while kissing her on her neck and making his way down to her breasts. He licked both of her brown nipples as they continued to get hard.

When Mitch made his way down south, he exercised his tongue in and out of amber's clitoris, causing her thighs to tighten up. She held and squeezed the pillows that were on the bed every time Mitch sucked on her clit, causing him to have an erection. Mitch then slid her black and pink tight boy shorts down that were squeezing all of her round ass that was complimenting her all black Victoria Secret bra. He then slid all of his manhood into her while spooning.

After a couple of strokes, amber couldn't take enough and went down on Mitch and sucked all of his nine inches. Amber licked around the shaft of his dick while spitting and slurping every drop of cum that he shot directly into her mouth without causing a drop to drip from her mouth.

"You like that, daddy?" amber said in her sexy tone while sucking all the evidence of cum down her throat. She then moved on to his balls.

"Yes, mama, si."

Mitch's toes started to curl in his socks as he started to bite his bottom lip.

Not long after, amber was fast asleep. She left Mitch up twisting a dutchee to smoke before passing out with Amber.

"Damn, I love this girl to death," Mitch thought to himself as he gazed at amber while she slept peacefully. He then before turned off his lamp that rested on his nightstand.

"God has truly blessed me with the woman of my dreams," Mitch thanked the man above for bringing him Amber...

June 12th, 2014

3:45 PM

"Yo, homie, you got a 50 double up? I only have 42 dollars with ten dollars in all quarters," asked a feind.

"Yeah, and next time have all the cash with you," Mitch said as he handed the fiend the 50 double up of crack rock.

As the fiend walked away and bent the corner, Mitch's cell started to ring. When he looked at it, it was C Mac.

"Yo, what's up, cuz? Where you at?" Mitch asked.

"Shit, murda, I'm right here at the Del Amo Swap Meet, copping some earrings. What you got poppin?" c mac asked in return.

"Aye yo, homie, ain't you Mitch's homeboy?" asked a young slim dude named Brandon.

"Yeah, that's him," said another young soldier accompanying Brandon.

"Fuck yall bitch ass niggas and fuck Squarehood, this Brick Boyz Crip!" brandon shouted at c mac with Mitch listening in on the phone.

"Nigga, what? Fuck all y'all and ya dead homies!" c mac snapped back while withdrawing one of his 9mm glocks from his waistband.

"What y'all bitch ass niggas wanna do?" Mitch challenged the two young crips on while the other shoppers were watching.

"I'm by myself, y'all some bitch ass niggas," c mac said with death in his voice while cracking a smile. Just as the two young crips withdrew their weapons, they were interfered by the two security guards. The guards forced the two to leave the swap meet before they called the Long Beach Police.

"We'll catch you and Mitch later," Brandon said as he gave c mac a gun gesture to his head, signaling that things would end up in gun smoke.

"What was that all about? you good, C Mac?" Mitch asked while dumping out the dutchee guts into his trash bin.

"Yeah, it was just them young dumb mothafuckas Brandon and one of his little homies threatening me and you with death, saying that he was gonna kill us," c mac said.

"Yeah, a lot of people wanna see me down and out behind bars and all," Mitch said with light chuckle. "Fuck them niggas, though. We just gotta move in silence, keep our eyes open, and don't get caught slipping," said Mitch before hanging up his receiver and taking some long drags from his dutchee that he just twisted up.

5:37 PM

"Yo, cuz, fuck all them niggas, we gonna teach them all a lesson. Pass me that gas can," brandon said to his young soldier while exiting out his Buick beelining towards one of Mitch's rock houses.

"We gonna burn this mothafuckin crack house down and bring c mac and Mitch bitch ass's to us," Brandon said while pouring gasoline all around one of Mitch's dope houses.

"Light up a Newport and pass it to me," Brandon took a couple of puffs of the menthol and flicked the cigarette onto the ground, causing a fiery flame that brought the house into a fireball.

"Let's go to the store and get us a bottle of Hennessy and wait till these bastards come to us," brandon said with a chuckle and smirk across his face. "Lets shake the spot before the firefighters and police come," said brandon as him and his young solider hopped in their ride and started the engine and then shot into traffic.

7:00 PM

"Yo, Mitch, them punk ass niggas burned down one of our rock houses," Tank shouted through the phone at Mitch.

"Yeah? You know who did it?"

"Yeah, some of the kids on the block said it was a green Buick with light tint leaving the block with niggas that looked like they were from the Briccs," Tank responded while looking at the fiery scene.

"Yeah, I bet you it was them little niggas brandon and his homies. They got into it with c mac at the swap meet earlier," Mitch said as he remembered being on the phone with C Mac while he was arguing with the Bricc Boyz. "We going to have to send them bitches to hell and send the

THE BUST   STANLEY JAMES II

projects a little message, you feel me, cuz?" Mitch
said with vengeance in his voice.

"Yeah, I feel you, loco, just tell me what you
want me to do and it's done," Tank said while
standing behind the yellow tape, on foot, at the
scene as the firefighter's were out doing their job
taking down the fire.

"Just gather a couple of homies together and
go put in that work for me. You know what to do
and where to ditch the car and guns, right?" asked
Mitch.

"Yeah, no problem, loco. I'm a call you in a
few with more details," Mitch said.

"Alright, bet," Mitch replied before hanging
up his cell phone.

After hanging up, Mitch pulled out his cell
phone and dialed c mac while pouring himself a
shot of Remy Martin. On the third ring, c mac
answered.

"Waddup?"

"Tank is gonna handle them niggas for you, so just kick back and meet me at my crib later on tonight so we can talk about opening another rock house for Tank and adding a couple of more muscles," Mitch said.

"Fuck that, I wanna be the one who kill that bastard!" C Mac said in a angry tone as he admired his twin glocks.

"Your time will come, trust me, we don't need anymore heat on us, especially with the FEDS on our tail. We got Beputy Boxer wanting to bring us down and Roddy locked up. We don't need anymore heat coming down on us, you feel me, loco?" Mitch was trying to get through his trigger happy comrade's head.

"Yeah, I hear you, murda. I'm a grab a bottle of yak and swing through less than an hour," C Mac said. He needed a drink with all the drama that was taking place around him.

"I'ght, fasho." Mitch hung up.

"Yo, come outside, I'm in the front, murda," c mac said as he was pulling up in front of Mitch's crib.

"You got some cups and a couple of Backwoods?" asked Mitch as he sat in the passenger seat pulling out a 100 sack of that sticky icky.

"C'mon, cuz, you know I stayed prepared," said c mac as he turned down the volume on his stereo that was playing the sounds of Young Jeezy and E-40 All The Same.

"I've been checking out this house for us to push from on Butler Street," said Mitch as his cell phone broke the conversation, reading tank's name across the caller ID.

"Yo, what's the word?" Mitcha asked.

"We went through the projects, me and Little Lowboy, and burned down two of their stash spots and shot the two niggas that hang with that bitch nigga Brandon," Tank said, feelinf accomplished.

"Good work, now the ball's in his court. Good looking out, I'm a set you up in your new spot to push from," said Mitch.

"I'ght, no doubt. I'ma get wit yall tomorrow," Tank replied.

"I'ght, bet," Mitch replied before hanging up.

"Who was that calling in, loco?" c mac asked while twisting up a couple of Backwoods of that sticky icky that Mitch had given him.

"Shit, it was tank. He said that he took care of that business and sent them fools in the projects a message," Mitch took a sip of his Remy Martin. "That nigga tank and little lowboy burnt down two stash houses and sent a couple of them niggas to meet their maker," Mitch said with a couple of chuckles after.

"Thats right, even though I wanted that nigga's head myself."

"You'll have your chance in due time, Crip, trust me. Let's just take it one day at a time," Mitch said as he reclined in the passenger seat, turning up the record 50 Cent God Gave me Style, God Gave Me Grace. He took a couple more drags of his Backwood before passing it to c mac.

8:30 PM

"Yo man, I swear to God Mitch and his whole crew is going down. I'm going to put a bullet in between Mitch's eyes for all that him and his crew has been doing," said a revengeful Deputy Boxer. "Them cocksuckas are going to have to pay with their freedom and lives for Thruman's death," boxer explained to his new partner Eric Gomez. "Just wait, I'm going to have their ass so screwed that Johnnie Cochran's son couldn't help them out," he hissed to Gomez while he was drinking a cold beer.

"Let's go ride up on brandon and see if he has anything useful information for us said," deputy boxer as they made their way to their unmarked car. "That's all they would ever be in life is black niggers who can't see that their doing our jobs for us by killing one another," deputy boxer said while pulling off into traffic.

"These mothafuckas kill each other every day and night for what, a simple color of a fucking block to sell dope on," Officer Gomez chimmed in and said.

"These niggers will never learn until it's too late. Well, fuck, all we have to do is sit back and let them kill off each other while we get paid," deputy boxer laughed as he placed a Marlboro between his lips and lit up the tip.

Deputy Boxer pulled into the project's parking structure directly in front of Brandon's crib. He was standing outside with three of his soldiers looking on in the background as they stopped from their dice game.

"So, what you got for us?" Deputy Boxer asked boldly

"Shit, why y'all pulling up like this at my crib with my homies out front?" brandon asked with uncertainty written on his face.

"What you scared for? You a tough gang member, right?" gomez said while trying to hold his laugh but couldn't.

"Yeah, whatever, muthafucka," brandon hissed back as he was putting his money in his back pocket. "Shit, Mitch and them Squarehood niggas done burnt down two of my stash houses, leaving your count kinda short," brandon said while tossing boxer 2,500 dollars in a white envelope.

"What the fuck do that has to do with my money?" snarled Deputy Boxer as he skimmed through the money for the correct amount.

"That nigga Mitch messed up your count, not me, and why you didn't take care of our problem?" Brandon asked and took his Newport Long from his pocket along with his BIC lighter.

"Look, that's your problem, but seems like you can't handle it yourself. Seems like I need to intervene, especially since it's messing up my money," boxer said to brandon with a stare that says your a fuck up.

"So, what about that fool Roddy? I heard he is going away for life in the can," brandon said with a smile.

"Yeah, that black bastard is going to rot in a prison cell until he dies, and for that bastard Mitch, I'm going to take care of him myself," boxer said while putting his car in drive and taking off, leaving a heavy cloud of dust in brandon's face causing him to cough.

"Fucking pigs!" said brandon as he placed his Newport between his lips and lit it.

"Everything okay, bos?" one of Brandon's soldier's asked from behind.

"Yeah, everything cool, cuz, jus get back in there and tell them bitches to bag up the weed for sale," Brandon puffed his cigarette and headed back to the dice game.

June 13th, 2014

11:14 AM

"Can you meet me at Sal's Gumbo Shack in about 30 minutes?" Rafel asked.

"No doubt, I'll be there," Mitch replied as he grabbed his 44. Eagle and keys from off the counter top and headed for the door.

"Is everything okay?" Mitch asked Rafael who was sitting at the table close to the window with his bodyguard close in reach.

"Yeah, I wanted to meet with you so we can talk about business," Rafel said while pouring cream and sugar into his coffee.

"I'm listening," Mitch took a seat, joining Rafel.

"So you know that I've been supplying Roddy and he has been supplying your crew and with him being locked up, I wanna go into business with a smart young leader such as yourself," Rafael said. "For now on, I will supply you, give you and your crew some of the best lawyers in the country, and give you a little more muscle. I did some research and found out that you and your crew are being investigated by the FBI and also I found out that a deputy by the name of Boxer has a hit out on you, so with that being said, seems like you don't really have much of a choice but to partner with me," rafel stated while taking some sips of his coffee.

"Yeah that sounds pretty legit," Mitch said as he tried to signal over the young waitress.

"Is there anything I can get you?" the young waitress asked.

"Yeah, I'll take a breakfast sandwich with some orange juice," Mitch said.

"Okay, I'll be back with your food shortly," the waitress said. She then walked off toward the kitchen.

"So do we have a partnership?" rafel asked while extending his hand out.

"Yes indeed," Mitch replied while shaking his hand.

"Good, i'll call you in a couple of days with the packages," Rafel got up and made his way to the exit with his macho bodyguard walking behind him.

The waitress then reappeared with Mitch's food."Here you go, sir, is that all for you?" she asked.

"Yes ma'am, that's all," he took his food to-go and paid his tab. He also left a twenty dollar tip before he made his swift exit.

As Mitch sat in his BMW, he replayed all the possible scenarios that could happen in the future. He sat back and twisted up a blunt of OG and started his engine. He then shot into traffic, he was feeling accomplished.

June 14th, 2014

8:37 AM

"So how much time I'm looking at?" asked a nochanlant Roddy while sitting back in his steel chair handcuffed by the wrists.

"Well, Mr. Stevenson, they're charging you with 1st degree murder of a police officer, attempted murder on a police officer with a deadly weapon along with that 100 grams of powder cocaine and weapons they found in your vehicle," said his lawyer Mr. Sanchez. "To be frank, you would be looking at a possible 30 to 75 years if they don't give you the death penalty," Sanchez added as he fixed his checkered colored tie.

"Fuck it, you do the crime, you do the time," Roddy said and took a sip of his coffee with his free hand.

"Do what you have to do to get me off this death penalty, I've already done a four hundred year prison sentence in my mind, I can do six hundred more," Roddy said nonchalantly as he sat his cup of Spades coffee back onto the steel table. "Did you speak to Mitch yet?" Roddy asked Mr. Sanchez while looking into his eyes.

"Yeah I spoke to him and he said to hold your head up and that he will continue to run the business. He also said that he met up with Rafael for business."

"Cool, I figured it would only be a matter of time before he met my connect because sooner or later, I was going to introduce him to Rafael," Roddy took another sip of his coffee.

"Well okay, is there anything else you need me to take care for you on the outside?" asked mr. sanchez.

"Yeah, as a matter of fact, there are a couple of more things I need you to handle," he said while eyeing him. "First, I need you to go and give my family some money to continue paying the bills and to keep food on the table," said Roddy as he wrote down the numbers to his bank and accountant. "Secondly, I need for you to send me some books and magazines while I wait this bitch out," Roddy said in a unpleasant tone. He was bored in his cell and he needed some kind of entertainment.

"Okay, I will handle all of your requests first thing in the morning. Is there anything else I can do for you?"

"Nah, that is it and I appreciate everything you have been doing for me over these past years," Roddy said with sincerity in his voice.

Their meeting was shortly abrupted by the C.O coming in and telling Roddy that his visiting time had expired.

4:15 PM

"Man, where the fuck are these bitch ass niggas?" hissed an impatient c mac.

The duo had been driving for hours through the projects. They were in a stolen black Acura looking for Brandon and his foot soldiers.

"These little niggas hiding out," Mitch said while gripping his 50. CAL Desert Eagle while checking around the projects in the blind spots that civilized people didn't know about.

Little did C Mac and Mitch know, they were being tailed and photographed by the FBI. They were about four cars behind in an unmarked white Dodge pickup truck.

"So, what's the plan?" asked the trigger happy c mac as he was twisting up a Backwood in with one hand and the other on the steering wheel.

THE BUST STANLEY JAMES II

"Shit, these niggas are in hiding," c mac laughed outrageously.

"Fuck it then, cuz, I'm hungry, let's get some Jack in the Crack on 52nd and Atlantic," suggested a calm Mitch.

"Fuck it, i'm cool with that," c mac answered back. He then turned up the radio in the stolen Acura, playing the song Crip Hop by Snoop Dogg and Tha Eastsidaz.

"Man, turn that shit down, cuz, there goes them bitch ass niggas right there, on Crip," Mitch said as he made sure his 50. CAL was locked and loaded with his extra clip in his backpocket. Mitch made a hindi exit up the side of the stolen Acura unseen.

"Thanks for ordering with us. Please come again," the lady cashier at Jack in the Box said. She gave Brandon and three of his foot soldiers their bags of food and the three men exited.

"Yo cuz, what the fuck yall ordered?" asked one of the foot soldiers. He was wearing a Atlantic

Ave shirt, that represented their turf, in big bold block lettering. He walked out holding the door for Brandon with the others right on the back of his heels.

"I ordered some curly fries and a bacon burger and hell no, yall can't have any of my curly fries," Brandon said.

Brandon was the first to walk out the restaurant to come to his fate.

"Aye Crip, where you from again?" was the only thing brandon heard as he looked up. he was then greeted with the flash of Mitch's 50. CAL Desert Eagle being the last thing he ever saw.

The three soldiers that were with brandon saw his body hit the pavement in a split instance. They tried to withdraw their pistols from their waistbands but was a minute too late. C Mac spit out multiple rounds from his twin glocks. He dropped two instantly and hit the third man in the shoulder and leg, sending him flying back into Jack in the Box.

Pop pop, pop!

Gun shots filled the Jack in the Box parking structure. Pedestrians and kid's ran to take cover from the rain of bullets that c mac was spitting. He continued to shoot into the Jack in the Box entrance door, not caring about any innocent people being shot. The third wounded soldier fled back inside for cover.

"Fuck nigga, don't nobody go against the hood and especially when it comes to my money," C Mac kicked Brandon in the face numerous of times as he laid in his own pool of blood that was overflowing into the street.

"Let's get out of here," Mitch shouted.

They both ran back towards the stolen Acura. They hopped in and punched on the gas, putting the petal to the metal the only way he knew how.

They swerved lane to lane trying to hop onto the 91 freeway heading West. The song on the radio was playing Lil Boosie Badass Long Clips and

Choppers. At that moment, c mac seemed to notice a unmarked Dodge pickup truck that seemed to be tailing them closely.

"Yo cuz, I think that is the FEDS on us," c mac said, pointing them out to Mitch in his rearview mirror.

Mitch turned his neck to see the van behind them. "Fuck, I know they been trailing us all morning and I know they seen us dump them project niggas out. What we gonna do?" C Mac asked as he began to sweat. He was now panicking.

"Just keep cool, try to lose them and then get off on Alameda. Drop me off so I can ditch the guns and split up," Mitch said as he tried to keep his cool for C mac. He knew if he got amped up, C Mac would panick even more.

"Nah cuz, you can ditch your gun but i'm keeping my babies," c mac said while switching from lane to lane as they tried to lose the pickup truck.

"I'ght, good, we lost them for now. They're about ten cars behind us," c Mac said as he exited the freeway.

"Shit, I'm good right here by this canal," Mitch said as he hopped out the stolen Acura. He gave daps to his comrade and bailed down the canal. He then threw his hot 50 CAL. into the current water flow. C mac sped off doing 100 miles per hour like he was on a Nascar straight away track.

Not soon after, the FEDS gained back their presence only being about three cars behind. C Mac knew they were still on his tail trailing him, they gained up on him quickly.

"Fuck!" C Mac shouted as he drove over 100 miles down Artesia Blvd with the FEDS on hot pursuit. The byrd (helicopter) now started to hover above.

"Pull over!" C Mac heard over the PA system from the hovering byrd (helicopter) above.

Before he knew it, C Mac started to pull to the right. The driver door swung open, that's when C Mac made a mad dash through the industrial buildings as he let off a couple of rounds towards the FBI's direction.

C Mac was hopping wall from wall, gate to gate as the bryd (helicopter) tried to keep up with his movements. Sirens were coming from everywhere. Even all the local news crews and journalists were in attendance trying to get one of the biggest gang related stories in Long Beach California under their belt.

"Fuck, this is some bullshit!" C Mac shouted as he pinned crouched down behind a garbage dumpster. He then reloaded both of his twin glocks until he heard the clicking sound, signaling that they were locked and loaded and ready to go out western cowboy style.

"We have you surrounded!" said one of the Federal Agents over the loudspeaker.

The rest of the Federal Agents then gathered around him and took their perimeter with all their weapons pointed directly at the garbage dumpster. Deputy Boxer and the rest of the local Sheriff's arrived on scene to give aid.

The first thing that ran through C Mac's mind was to call Mitch and tell him that it was over for him. He peeled out his cell phone and dialed Mitch's number. "Yo, where you at, you good?" Mitch asked afer he answered on the first ring with the wind blowing in his background.

"Yo murda, they got me cornered on Artesia in these factories behind this dumpster," C Mac said as he wiped the sweat from his forehead with the bottom of his shirt.

"Get out of town now, murda, I'm not going out without a blaze and you know they comin for you next once they find out who I am and that we have ties," c mac huffed as his voice started breaking.

"Fuck, homie, I love you, cuz," Mitch said. Multiple gunshots was the last thing he heard before looking at the screen of his trap phone. He then hung up and tossed it into the canal further down as he bailed.

"Fuck, this is it, cuz, I'm going to enjoy this shit." C Mac twisted up his last Backwood and put flame to the tip. He exhaled and blew out the remaining smoke that was in his mouth. He blew it into the sky blue air. That's when he saw a 92.3 The Beat radio station blimp reading the famous quote by 50 cent "Get Rich or Die Trying. He reloaded and checked his twin glocks before jumping from behind the dumpster and letting off his two clips.

"Fuck the police, this crip! We don't die, we multiply!"

"Cuz, this shit is all messed up," was what Mitch was telling himself as he bailed down half a mile and caught a nearby passing taxicab to his hood with a lot on his mind.

"Yo, cuz, y'all all over the scanner," Tristan said as soon as he saw Mitch exiting the taxi cab and walking up Scott Street a couple of houses down from his pop's crib.

"Yeah? Have you heard anything about c mac?" Mitch asked with so much eagerness in his tone.

"Yeah, he was captured after a hour long shootout with the FEDS. The scanner said he was hit four times, once in the shoulder, twice in the thighs, and once in the hand but they captured him after he was shot. They are taking him to Downtown LA to the federal jail emergency room. The scanner been mad crazy, I'm pretty sure it's on the news. It is gonna be extremly hot around this mothafucka now," Tristan said as he made a slang to a neighborhood feind named Pittsburg.

Pittsburg cracked his smile, showing his messed up grill that was missing his front teeth as the 100 sack of rock cocaine was dropped into his dirty palms. Quickly, the crackhead disappeared on his bike in 6th gear like he was never there.

"Yeah, fosho, good looking out big homie. I think I'm just going to go ahead and take the family out to Washington DC so I can go check out that historically black college Howard and register while I let shit calm down around here, you know?"

"Yeah cuz, that's probably your safe bet. You need to get the fuck from around here," said Tristan. "Remember when I was on the run and I went to New York on tour with the hottest group Wu-Tang for about 11 months," said a Veteran OG Tristan.

Tristan knew all so well about the life of crime, he was a true seasoned Crip that Mitch looked up to and learned majority of his street and dope game from.

"I'll hold everything down around here while you're gone," Tristan stated as he pulled out a camel hump from his back pocket and lit the tip.

Their conversation was interrupted by Tristan's cell phone ringing. It was Roddy calling from the Los Angeles County Jail. On the first ring, Tristan answered.

"Waddup, Crip, what it's, looking like in there murda?"

"Awe, mane, the little homies names are ringing already, cuz," Roddy wholeheartedly said with a smile and heavy chuckle right after.

"Yeah, I know they going crazy all over the scanner, as a matter of fact, cuz, Mitch is right here right now as we speak," Tristan said.

"Yeah? Let me speak to him, murda," Roddy asked while looking at all the other inmates in there waiting to use the phone.

Tristan handed Mitch the cell phone.

"What up, crip? How many pushups can you do now?" Mitch asked while cracking a small laugh.

"Shit, you know, about 450 already," Roddy laughed. "Nah, but on some other shit, you and C

Mac's name is already ringing hard in this muthafucka, you hear me, loco? You and your little niggas is doing y'all shit is all I can say. Seems like yall done picked up a little too early on this street shit. Y'all got the street's and the prisons talking, saying y'all with that bullshit and will lay a pig down if y'all have to. That's the word through the grapevine," Roddy said as he now watched the movements of the CO's.

"Well, you know what we all signed up for, Crip. We live by the gun, we die by the gun," Mitch said with loyalty in his heart and dedication in his tone.

"Yeah, you is right, Crip. I just wish me and your big homie Tristan was smart enough to tell y'all not follow our footsteps, but hey, what can I say that's life, right?' Roddy said, showing off his wisdom.

"You have one minute left," was the message that flashed between their conversation.

"well, shit, we about to hit the chow hall. I'll holla at y'all on count, be safe and love yall, murda," said Roddy.

"Tips, we gonna put ten g's on your books in the am, murda," Mitch replied before hanging up the cell phone and handing it back to Tristan.

"I'm about to go make this slang over the bridge real quick and get a pack camel humps because that was my last one I smoked," Tristan said before heading over towards his jet black 2013 Lexus that was parked across the street.

"You love fucking with them otb feinds," chuckled Mitch as he watched Tristan head towards his car.

"You know I go where ever for that paper, I don't give a fuck about no otb. Shit, that's y'all generation, shit," Tristan laughed as he started his Lexus. He gave life to his engine and then gave daps to Mitch as he slid off into traffic with the sounds of Pusha T's latest song Numbers on The Board, screaming through his stereo speakers.

"My nigga," Mitch shook his head and walked down to his pop's crib. As he was walking, he saw his homeboy Scrap Loc pulling up aside of him.

"North up, crip, what you got cracking?" Scrap Loc asked.

"Shit, about to head in and see what pop's talking about. What you got going?" he asked right after.

"Shit, I came through because I wanted to see if you wanted to push with me to the homie Vince Staples show tonight at the Kodak theatre in downtown LA, crip. We got a couple of backstage passes and all," Scrap Loc said with his same childhood smile that he wore when the two of them first met in junior high school.

"Yeah, that's going to be cracking, we up in that thang," Mitch replied while breaking a smile.

"Well shit, no doubt. You wanna drive or roll with the homies and bitches in the limousine?"

"Shit cuz, what you mean? We in our state, the

homie performing we gonna do it big tonight. We in the limo," Mitch said, now fully smiling his pearly whites.

"Aight cuz, the limo gonna be here tonight around 10:30 pm."

"I'ght, that's cool, bet," Mitch gave Scrap Loc daps and then headed towards the front door.

10:30 PM

Honk, honk! Mitch heard a horn blowing along with loud music and laughter coming from the limousine outside.

Mitch was dressed down in his True Religion white and black shirt with his black True Religion jeans to match and his all-black Polo boots to accompany his fit. He had a couple of gold chains that dangled with charms as well as his gold 24k bracelet with his Movado watch to set it off. As he walked towards the door, he grabbed his 44. desert eagle and put it in his waistband, undetected.

He walked towards the front to door and stopped. He went to go check on his pop's. when he walked into the living room, his father was sitting back drinking a beer, and watching his favorite old Western's that showed in black and white. Mitch's father knew all about his dealings and his reputation out there in the street's, but that didn't seem to matter much , he still looked at him as his son.He taught his son well about the pro's and con's of the street life, primarily joining gangs.

"Are you good? Is everything all right? You need anything, pop's?" Mitch asked as he straightened up the pillows that he was prompted on.

"Nah, I'm good, son, just be careful out there, okay?" he said with that fatherly love tone.

"Alright, pop's. I'll be back later on to check up on ya," Mitch pecked his pops on the forehead and placed several 50's and 100 dollar bills into his left front shirt pocket aand he headed out the front door, locking it behind him.

" Yo, you ready, north?" Scrap Loc said. He hopped out the limo dressed down in his cutthroat attire with his matching brown high top Air Forces. He stepped out and he gave Mitch a dap followed with a hug.

"Hell yeah!" Mitch replied. He grabbed the Ace of Spade bottle of champagne from Scrap Loc and started guzzling the bubbly beverage down, immediately feeling the rich drink.

When he stepped a foot into the limousine, he saw some familiar faces. He saw the Allie Crips members Slim65. He has a skinny body frame that held up all his gold chains. He saw gebo, he did a brief county stint as cellmates. A couple of hot girls was from the hood were there enjoying the festivities. They knew being from the ghettos of Long Beach, it was very rare that an average person rode around in a luxury limo with champagne liquor, weed, and powder at their fingertips.

Big money was sitting in the limousine as they all enjoyed their ride down the 10 Freeway towards the theater. They were bumping the song Fetty Wap RGF Island through the limousine stereo as loud as the knob could turn. Bottles of all different kinds of liquor were being passed around along with a 100 sack of powder. Several partygoers indulge in the powder before they pulled up to the theater. Through the back entrance they all went through, they met up with rapper and homies Vince Staples and joey fats. They all had backstage passes hanging around their neck.

"Y'all good?" asked Vince staples. He was to perform with Joey Fatts, Asap Rocky, and Mac Miller.

"Yeah, we good, homie," Scrap Loc replied.

"Well check this out, I'm performing next, cuz. Y'all come on stage with me," he gave Mitch the head nod.

Vince Staples put his earplugs in and grabbed his microphone. He then walked on stage along with Mitch, Scrap Loc, and the homies that were there in attendance to support their friend.

The music was blasting full volume as Mitch and Scrap Loc were on stage. They were waving their bottles of bubbly champagne in the air as Vince Staples ripped his verse to the full capacity crowd.

With all the cameras and recorders that were on stage recording, little to Mitch's surprise, it was the hip-hop FEDS taking pictures of Mitch while he was on stage living the rock star life. Each day that went by, the tried to put together a strong enough case to put Mitch and his gang behind bars for life, but they could never catch Mitch touching dope.

Mitch was having the time of his life and a night to never forget. He had met up with all the big time rapper's, actors, and entertainers. He took many pictures until he heard someone from the distance say, "Mitch, is that you, man? I read your manuscript, and cuz, I felt it from the heart!" said an unfamiliar face that was slowing approaching as he continued to talk. "You might not know me yet, but my name is Chris Davis. I'm the CEO Chief Editor and Publisher for MTV Books and your manuscript somehow made it to my desk. It was referred by an old colleague who teaches at Compton College named Mrs. Basset. She complimented you, she said you had real talent and a real story to tell but was just caught in your past," Chris Davis said. "I gave it a read and loved it!" He walked over and shook Mitch's hand. "I felt your story deeply from the heart. I can say you got something here, sir. I wanna talk to you about some business some other time." He handed his personal business card with his personal cell phone number on it to Mitch." Give me a call, you might have a future out there in New York," Mr. Davis said as he walked away sipping his light drink before disappearing in the crowd backstage.

The Hip Hop Police cameras and recorders caught everything on tape that night backstage with the infamous gangsta Crip Mitch. He actually hated being in the forefront of cameras and being put in the spotlight, but he didn't care that night, he was too high on cocaine, weed, and liquor that he had in the limo.

Moments later, within the same room backstage, there was a commotion going on in the corner. Several guys where mercilessly stomping a guy out that Mitch couldn't put a face to. As Mitch walked closer, he saw it was Slim 65, Gebo, and Tiny Loco. They were stomping the life out of a young Crip by the name of Little Manic. He was from Brick Boy Crips. The Brick Boys were there to support his homie from his turf that was rapping earlier that night.

Mitch ran over and joined in kicking him like a rag doll. They stomped him until he was unconscious. After they were finished stomping him out, he was awakened by the security guards. They had to escort him out with their guns drawn to their sides for the safety of Little Manic, once outside.

Mitch Scrap Loc and all the other young gangstas hurried out the back door. They ran to the limo that was parked on the side of the theater with the engine still running. They all hopped in with laughter, they didn't have a care in the world. They cruised through the Hollywood and the Beverly Hills area. They were enjoying the scenery on their way to the after party.

As the limousine stopped at the light on the corner of Washington Blvd, all gangstas in the limo removed their guns from their waistbands when they saw the car behind slowly creeping up behind them with four people in the car behind them. An all-white cocaine Chevy Impala pulled on to the right side of the limousine. The back left side passenger window rolled down, revealing the swollen face Little Manic. He drew his 40. caliber pistol and shot all eleven rounds into the side of the limousine and shattered all the windows. He didn't have a specific target but he wanted to hit and kill anything his bullets found.

Pop pop, pop!

The side window on the limousine shattered all over the backs of everybody in the limo.

"Fuck, who is that?" Slim 65 shouted as he was ducked down to avoid the hot bullets that was being shot at the limo.

"It's that nigga Little Manic," Gebo replied as he shot off two rounds at the escaping Impala.

"Chase that motherfucka instructed!" Scrap Loc shouted to the driver.

The driver put his foot to the gas and started to give chase.

Boom, boom! was the sounds of Mitch's 44. desert eagle with returned fire coming his way.

Pop, pop! Scrap Loc shot his 45. as the Impala dipped through traffic and escaped onto the freeway.

"Fuck them, we gonna catch them bitch ass niggas later on. They on the list now," said Scrap Loc. He was referring to all their main enemies who they shed blood with and soldiers dying from both sides due to gang violence that overfilled the streets of Long Beach and Los Angeles County city wide.

"Drop us off at my car," said Scrap Loc. "Someone gotta die tonight," he continued with fire in his eyes.

Mitch suddenly began to think about MTV's CEO Chief Editor and publisher Chris Davis. He remembered that he had his personal business card and told him that he would contact him later on about doing business.

Mitch spoke up and said, "drop me off at my car too, I'm going to take care of this one on my own on, Crip," Mitch said as he took out his weed and Dutchmaster.

"Fasho, I can understand, Crip," Scrap Loc said while looking into Mitch's eyes. They were like brothers so he respected his wishes, knowing that he really liked to do dirt alone or with his roll dog C Mac who was now federally incarcerated. "Take my man's to his car," said Scrap Loc as he took a pull from his already lit Backwood that was consuming the air in the limousine. Minutes later, he was pulling up to his BMW that sat like a million bucks, in the early morning hours, in front of Coolidge park.

"Yo, cuz, I'll fuck with yall later on," Mitch said. He gave each Crip a dap and hug. He then told them north up as he got into his ride and put the key in the ignition. The limousine pulled off down the street to hop in traffic.

Mitch sat there in silence with the key in the ignition while replaying all the events that transpired that night. He thought about everything that took place. He remembered seeing his homies perform live and being backstage meeting a gang of celebrity's, athletes, and entertainers. He remembered meeting the CEO Chief Editor Chris Davis then mercilessly stomping out Little Manic, and having a drive by and Midnight Street shootout with him right after.

As Mitch sat there, he turned on the stereo and played 50 Cent's song God Gave Me Style, God Gave Me Grace. He sat there and twisted himself a honey dutchee and sipped on a small bottle of Avion Tequila that he pulled from the side of his car. After finishing his blunt and dumping the roach into the ashtray, he pulled off and drove in front of his pop's crib. When Mitch pulled up, the FEDS were sitting in an unmarked white Charger in front of his pop's house, directly across the street in clear view.

Before pulling all the way up, Mitch stopped quickly and through his gears in reverse and backed up two houses down from his pops house. Mitch started to low key panic and had flashbacks of the authorities closing him in, he felt some anxiety coming on.

"Fuck, cuz, I gotta get out here first thing next week. I just have to make a couple of moves and stack a couple of more bands so me and the family can make this move," said a spooked Mitch. He drove down a couple of blocks and parked in a far parking structure close to the freeway on Coolidge Park. He parked and fell into a deep sleep

with the engine running along with his stereo
playing the late Chinx's song Fuck The Other Side.

June 15th, 2014

5:46 AM

Mitch was suddenly woken up from his deep high cocaine and liquor slumber by his cell phone ringing with Tristan's name across the screen. When he finally got his eyes opened, he realized where he was. He looked at the pediatricians that brought their dogs to the dog park early in the morning. They had their dog waste bags along with their pooper scoopers. he also seen some young sport athletes getting some running and workouts in before the sun had officially risen.

"Man, is all this shit what I'm fighting for, and what my brothers died for really worth it?" he asked himself before answering.

"Hello, Waddup, Crip? You still sleep with the birds chirping at yo ass at the park, huh?" Tristan asked with a laugh following.

Mitch looked around everywhere and couldn't seem to locate where Tristan was at, looking at him.

"Where the fuck you at, cuz? How you know I'm at the park, anyway, cuz?" Mitch asked in a jokingly manner.

"Cuz, I'm sitting in a tree looking at your ass. I'm everywhere, murda," Tristan replied back with his laughter growing. "Where you at, though?" Tristan asked. I need you to hit your Mexican plug for me so I can cop some work," Tristan added.

"Shit, I'm hot as a firecracker. I honestly don't think he gonna fuck with me right now, but fuck it, I'll try," said Mitch.

"Good looking out, Crip. I need eight of them thangs," he said into the receiver.

"Alright, I got you. I'm going to hit you on a little later today," replied Mitch before hanging up his end of the line.

8:30 AM

Mitch was playing the latest NBA 2K game with his son in the bedroom on his new Xbox 360. They were shouting and enjoying every minute of it as he splashed buckets all over his young son Nasir who didn't have a clue to what's was going on. All he knew that he loved to spend time with his father and enjoy his fun and laughter.

"What team you wanna play with next, son?" he asked as he sat down his controller and checked his text messages. His phone was blinking the blue light, indicating that he had an email message from Howard University. Mitch opened the email and began to read it. The email stated that he was receiving plane tickets for him and his family to attend the Historical Black College tour and registration event. They told him to bring his transcripts and all his writing material for the scholarships and grants that he qualified for through his academics testing. This was going to be a two week stay and all expenses were paid for. The only thing they needed was spending money and money for food which was not on campus. Nonetheless, that was not a problem for Mitch, he already had nearly 700 thousand dollars in a safe that was buried in his backyard under the pavement with his big George Foreman grill hiding his stash. It was hidden at beach house he had from a lucrative black market trade money that had ties to the Mexican Cartel. Mitch looked up with a huge cracked smile. He knew that the world could see that this young black male had been through the ringer and back especially at a young age.

Mitch then looked back towards his son, He was growing ever so big, every second of each day. He looked at his son with the biggest smile on his face that no one had ever seen. He looked at his son Nasir playing the basketball ball game and a single salty tear fell down his cheek. He wanted a better life and he wanted to be able to bring his son up in a better life than he grew up in.

He thanked the man upstairs with saying the Lord's Prayer as he rubbed the top of his son's head saying, "I love you, papi."

"I love you too, poppa," Nasir replied back with a warm hug and the biggest smile that could light up any room. he picked up his controller and pressed buttons as if he knew what he was doing.

"A nigga just need to make one more bust so I can flip it into a couple of bands really quick. After I make that move, I can head out to Washington DC so I can start a new chapter in my life and hopefully leave the game alone for a while," Mitch thought to himself. He knew that in this lifestyle he had chosen, there was no hanging up his Chucks and pistol forever. He thought of it as retiring from the streets and the dope game for a while. But, he knew that realistically, there was no outs due to how deep he was in the devil's game.

11:47 AM

Mitch took his BMW to the local car wash for a nice wash and detail. He decided to go to the car wash that everyone on the North went to just so they could be seen on Market and South Street. He turned into the parking structure with Gucci Mane's song Bricks subbing through the speakers. Mitch hopped out, grabbed his wallet, his book he was reading, his drink, and left his engine running. The Mexican wash tenant hopped in the driver's seat and pulled his BMW into the next available wash stall.

Within forty-five minutes, his car was brought out looking brand new as if it were fresh off the lot. It was deeply shampooed and detailed with their top quality wash. Mitch gathered his belongings and picked up his book titled The White House by one of his favorite authors Jaquavis Coleman. He threw the Mexican man who detailed his car a crisp blue face hundred dollar bill and said, "next time, amigo."

He hopped in and played his favorite song Picture me Rollin by the late Tupac Shakur. Times like this, he missed his homies that were going down by the day because of senseless drive-bys and gang killings like his little homies Baby Craze was. At the tender age of 14, he was gunned down over a dice game on the East Side of Long Beach and Little 4Shot died of a drug overdose in his sleep at his baby mother's house while laying on the couch. Then the incarceration of his big homie Roddy, his roll dog C Mac who was facing the death penalty, and now his main dope pusher Tank was caught up in a drug sting by a local crackhead. The crackhead agreed to set him up for a lighter sentence from being caught earlier that morning with a crack pipe and 8-ball in her possession. Her name was Cynthia, she was a middle-aged smoker who would do anything for her next high, even if it took putting someone behind bars as long as she got her fix.

Tank was caught while retrieving his dope from one of Mitch's delivery men. A few minutes after he did his pickup, he was raided by the FEDS, Deputy Boxer, and his team of turtles (sheriff's gang unit). He was caught with four bricks of pure, uncut cocaine, and two ounces of some MDA. He remained silent when they questioned and pressured him for any useful information pertaining to Mitch. Tank was a true rider, a loyal gangsta, and above everything else, he was an old school type of gangsta that was cut from a different cloth. He never mentioned a thing about Mitch or his ties to the Square Hood Crips. He took his 11 ½ years in the Federal Penitentiary of Lompoc like a real Mafioso gangster. The prison was located up north towards the Pacific Coast Ocean.

"Just keep a nigga book's fat," was all he asked for before receiving his lengthy sentence. He then threw up four fingaz with his thumb tucked.

Life as Mitch knew it was spiraling downwards quickly in a rapid pace, but he knew deep down in his heart that after contacting his Mexican connect Rafael, him and his family would be straight after this last time of copping and dumping off four kilos of cocaine that was estimated to be valued of 100 thousand dollar street value. Mitch couldn't wait for the remainder seventy-two hours before their flight took off to the other side of the country to experience something totally new. He knew that he would be much more of some help towards his family, his potna's back home, and the homies in those cell blocks, once he makes it right.

Mitch picked up his cell phone and slid his wallpaper screen over from his son and baby mother amber's face to the contact list. He skimmed through his contacts looking for Tristan's number. Once he found his number, he called him. Mitch didn't get an answer so he figured Tristan must have been knocked out or busy out somewhere making slangs. Mitch then went to the adjacent room and was abruptly interrupted by a call coming in from Chris Davis from MTV Books in New York City.

"Yo, hello? What's up?" Mitch asked after letting it ring three times. He was pacing back and forth in his makeshift office. He then started fixing his books on his library shelves. The shelves were filled with many books relating to African American History, science books, urban fiction books, and his favorite poetry books that he educated himself with since a young kid. His mother showed him the love for books when life was peaches and cream for a young Mitch. That was a time when Mitch had both of his parents in the same house under one roof as a loving caring family. But things had changed and time hasn't stopped for no one. The only person Mitch cared about in his young tender days was his mother. His mother had left him one night with his father and she never came back home that night. But that was another story.

"Hey there, how are things going for you? How's your writing coming along? Do you have any new projects?" he asked question after question in the most exciting tone that kind of have Mitch excited.

"Well, it's coming along really good. I'm about to drop my debut title The Bust (Live By The Gun Die By The Gun) under the West Coast Best-Selling Author Terry Wroten and his No Brakes Publishing company. I'm just trying to make a couple of moves before I take my family on a small vacation," Mitch replied to Chris.

Chris started jotting down notes of this young urban writer Mitch. He had hopes of having a sit down with him at his office in New York to discuss the possibly of making big power moves and a brighter future.

"Well, that's great too hear… well, I'm calling on such short notice because since I was referred by my colleague who said she was once your teacher, her name is Mrs. Basset. I've been secretly doing some research about you and your work ethics, and I think you would be a great asset to us here in the big apple."

"Yeah, you honestly think so?" Mitch asked in amazement.

"Yeah, from all the manuscripts and short stories Mrs. Basset emailed me, I was highly impressed with your pen game," Chris said as he gave a young black man compliments, not knowing his entire history and criminal underworld he ran. "I would love to fly you and your family down to have a face to face sit down and discuss a future for you here in New York. How does that sound?" Chris added.

"It sounds like a plan," said a happy Mitch who showed all his fronts. He grabbed the broken down weed from off his desk and dumped it into the empty swisher and twisted it in enjoyment.

"Well, sounds like a plan. You should be receiving your plane tickets with directions here to my office in about two weeks," chris said while sitting at his desk editing a manuscript.

"No doubt," Mitch replied. He hung up his cell phone, stepped back, lit his Swisher Sweet. He then looked at his son's picture that was hanging on the wall. He was enjoying his moment, taking in every moment and every second of the good news he just received.

Everything seemed to be falling right into place at the perfect time. Mitch and his family had been invented to the Big Apple just in time, on a business opportunity. He was going to meet up with Chris right after seeing what Howard University had to offer. He wanted to make sure if he wanted to attend or not.

Everything that goes up must come down. Deputy Boxer was conveying a plan to settle with Mitch.

2:46 PM

As Mitch was laying down on the couch, eating a pastrami pizza and drinking a vanilla coke while watching the movie The Act of Valor, he decided it was time to call his Mexican connect Rafael and see if he could cop four kilos of his purest raw uncut Colombian cocaine before leaving in the next couple of days.

He paused the movie to pick up his cell phone to call Rafael. He answered on the first ring. "Hello, amigo, how things?" he said with adrenaline in his tone. "I see it's kinda hot for you, my friend. I spoke to my political officials and they said they can keep the Sheriff's and Local Police Department off your ass, but not the FEDS."

The FEDS were a different ball game. Rafael and his circle didn't want no dealings with them, but that Lieutenant Boxer, he has a hard out for you. He's just been recently promoted to Lieutenant and word has it that he has payed local informants and dope fiends to kill you. The best advice I can give you is to lay low and go out of town for awhile," he said while clipping the ends of his Cuban Cigar. "Take the family out on a nice cruise or something. Go to Jamaica," Rafael said as he put flame to the tip of his Cuban.

"You right, Rafael," Mitch said. "I'm thinking about taking my family on a month vacation to Canada," Mitch lied to throw his true intentions off far left. "But first, I need to meet up with you and talk about buying real estate with you, cuz," buying real estate meant buying kilos of cocaine. "This will be my last time buying property from you for awhile because of my vacation I'm going on in the next couple of days. I'm going to leave my man Tristan in charge until I get back," said Mitch. Although, he really didn't have any intentions of coming back to take back over.

Mitch simply wanted to come back as a retired gang member who's trying to help and make a difference in his very own city that he once ran with his gang, causing many mommas to cry as they bury their son's due to gang violence or their daughters who are strung out on rock cocaine and many explicit other drugs that led them to the corner's to prostitute their once golden temples.

Mitch had to put all his feelings and frustrations to the side. He had to concentrate on the topic at hand about getting those kilos and turning them bricks into quick cash while trying to elude the now newly promoted Lieutenant Boxer and the FEDS, grasp that feels to be closing on him as Mitch tries to make it out to Howard University just in the nick of time.

"Ill supply to you this last time until you leave and let things calm down around here for awhile," he said as he pulled on his Cuban cigar.

"Meet me at the Motel 6 by the Carson Plaza off of Carson Street and Avalon about 6:30 pm sharp," he said before hanging up his Galaxy Note then placing it back on the counter as he felt his palms itching.

3:46 PM

"Man, Deputy Bradley, I can't wait till I catch that swinging monkey Mitch and let him meet his maker," said a crazed now Letinuant Boxer as he spinned the barrel cylinder to his chrome plated 38. Revolver. He had a devilish grin running across his face.

"I thought the mission was to arrest and have a solid enough case with evidence against Mitch and his crew, Tristan, and all their other homies who are stamped for life inside the gang files that seems to always land on the City Prosecutor's desk?"

"You can arrest him and play that good cop role if you want, but if I get to him first, I'm putting a bullet between his eyes," Boxer said while reaching down for his Marlboro cigarettes.

Deputy Bradley sat back and listened to the crazed Lieutenant. He kept eyeing his chrome 38. Special, only having visions of Tristan. He was out and about making drug money right up under their noses. Boxer ran across him in Corcoran State Prison while Tristan was doing some time there. He slashed Boxer's left side of his jawline with a box razor that was taped to a tooth brush in a convict riot. The cut forced him to receive nearly 200 stitches and of course, Mitch who he hated because he was who Tristan took in under his wing on the streets, teaching him the street and drug game early in life since he was young. Boxer murmured with fire in his eyes.

"I'm going to catch you black niggers!" Letinuant Boxer spat in disgust, lighting his Marlboro and taking a heavy pull. "Did you receive the black duffel bag from the trunk?" asked Boxer as he put his gun into his holster that was hanging from his shoulders.

"Yeah, i got it right here," said Deputy Bradley.

Bradley got in the passenger with the large gym bag resting on his lap. The two pulled off into traffic in their supervisor unmarked police Ford Taurus.

"What's all this for?" asked a newly recruit to the force. He pulled out two birds of cocaine and a pistol with the bodies of six gangsters around the city that Boxer had killed with on his job.

"We're gonna have someone plant these in the possession of Mitch so that can only leave Tristan out and I want him. This job isn't business for me, it's personal," he wanted the long time revenge on Tristan to be done by him.

6:30 PM Sharp

"Yo, I'm here," said Mitch as he pulled up into the back of the Motel 6 parking structure. This was where they did their regular drug trade at. He saw Rafael and two other of his personal bodyguards with him sitting in the front seat's of the sudan truck.

"What's up, Amigo?" Mitch said as he exited out his BMW. Gucci Mane's Trap House was spazzing through his two 15' speakers that were in his trunk rattling. "It's all there, no need to count it," said Mitch as he tossed a small backpack filled with dead presidents into the passenger seat onto the lap of one of his Mexican bodyguards.

"Good, I trust you," replied Rafael while vibing to his Latin music.

"Toss him the bag," he handed his bodyguard, who was sitting up front in the passenger seat, a gym bag filled with 4 pre wrapped kilos of his purest raw uncut cocaine.

When the bodyguard handed him the gym bag, the sudan truck took off immediately with

Latin music blasting through the speakers. Mitch watched the sudan disappear into traffic.

"Now all I have to do is drop the dope off at the rock house so little Herm can move it for me like he said. He has potential buyers already lined up waiting for his play."

Mitch got in his car and replayed the conversation he previously had with Chris Davis, his Mexican connect Rafael, and the thought of attending Howard University or any historically black college that Mitch had his mind set on. He wanted to someday retire from this street life he knew all so well.

Once Mitch made it back to his hood to meet up with little Herm, he was quickly surprised that it was a line full of crackheads waiting for little Herm to supply them with their fix. Mitch sat and lowered his seat as he watched for a minute at all the movements and how little Herm came and served each crackhead their fix like they were in a drive thru at Mc Donald's. Mitch's crack houses should have the sign hanging above each house stating a billion sold.

Mitch then hopped out his BMW, not noticing the FEDS were now parked at the end of the block. They were snapping and taking photos of Mitch as he hopped out his car with the gym bag containing his four kilos. He walked up to the front of the residence and was greeted by little Herm who was now running the spot while Tank was absent.

The FEDS had captured everything on camera. They had enough footage to build up a solid case against him and his gang.

"Yo, what up, crip?" Mitch said as he tossed the black gym bag into the arms of little Herm who was only at the age of 17. "How's it looking?" Mitch asked with enthusiasm.

"Shit, they love this new product we got," Little Herm replied. He just was happy to be in a position to make fast money.

"I got a new package for you," Mitch said. "It's four of them thangs, can you handle it?" Mitch asked, looking him directly in the eyes.

"Yeah, I got you, big homie," Little Herm said as he zipped up the gym bag and took it to the back room to have it broken down and re packaged.

"You seen Tristan around lately?" Mitch asked while taking out his sticky icky green and dutch master. He broke it down, dumped the guts, and begin to twist up.

"Nah, haven't seen him all morning. As a matter of fact, here he is pulling up now," said Little Herm who was looking out the window when Tristan pulled up two houses away from their rock house that was several blocks around the corner from where they stayed.

Tristan got out his Lexus smoking a Camel Hump and walked to the front entrance of the rock house. The FEDS got Tristan on camera and video also, his every movement. They are now had matching descriptions, putting faces with voices.

Tristan knocked twice. The door opened and he was greeted by Mitch. He opened the front door and welcomed Tristan in with a dap and hug.

"What's the deal, big homie?" Mitch asked. "What you got crackin?"

"Shit, just driving through the hood checking out traps, yall good?" he asked.

Meanwhile, outside, Cynthia was riding her bike trying to chase her high. She wanted another fix from earlier that was paid for by Leintuant Boxer to set up Tristan. He had her setting bugs and placing dope and guns in his Lexus. She was the only crackhead that could get close enough to Tristan to set him up without ever being detected. She rode her bike down the street from the rock house they were all at. She saw Tristan's Lexus parked a couple of houses down out of sight. She looked back at Deputy Bradley and lieutenant Boxer who were sitting in their unmarked Taurus at the South end of the block. They signaled for her to complete her mission by bugging his Lexus and placing the guns and dope in the back, under the passenger seat.

When Cynthia looked back, Lientunat Boxer gave her the head nod to carry on as she did. Cynthia rode her bike up to side of the Lexus looked around to see if anybody had been watching her. She opened the passenger door and slid the small bricks of cocaine right under his passenger seat along with the gun that had many murders under it's belt. Before leaving the scene, Cynthia closed the Lexus door and dropped a bug under the car. She hopped back on her 10-speed and pedaled away in a hurry, hoping to not have been seen with Lieutenant Boxer.

He smiled and nodded his head as an assurance that the FEDS, who were occupying the North end of the block, caught everything on camera and video tape.

"We have some dirty cops in the force, I see," said the young Federal Agent who couldn't possibly be over the age of 27

The young Federal Agent along with the rest of the Federal Agents on scene saw all of their moves with the lady crackhead. She was caught placing guns and dope in Tristan's Lexus for two local Sheriffs that was in the Gang Task Force.

"What you have cracking for tonight?" Mitch asked Tristan.

"Shit, it ain't no telling, murda, gotta go check on mom's in a little bit then go home and catch the rest of that Laker game. You know Kobe went for 63 points the other night at Madison Square Garden. Did you watch that game?" Tristan asked.

"Yeah cuz, we all watched it together, remember?" Mitch said while passing Tristan the lit dutchee of his finest sticky icky.

"Damn, you right, cuz, my bad I smoke too much weed," Tristan said while taking a heavy pull from the blunt. When he exhaled all of the smoke, it seemed to put everything at ease. He laughed and Little Herm and Mitch joined in.

Knock Knock Knock! was what interrupted the heavy laughter.

"Who is it and how much you got?" Little Herm yelled through the steel door that was bolted down with five lock bolts on the door.

"I got a hundred, can you help an old man out?" the crackhead yelled through the double doors.

"Yeah, I got you. Come around the side with your money already out," Little Herm said as he went to the back room and retrieve his order.

"Well shit, I'm about to split and catch up with yall later on. Tristan, I'm a holla," said Mitch as he made his way towards the front exit, leaving the blunt with Little Herm.

"Shit, I'm outta here too, crip," Tristan said, following Mitch out through the front entrance. He gave Little Herm dap and a hug,

"We gonna meet up later on tonight at the crib?" Mitch asked as he walked towards his BMW that sat in the sun like they were at a car show.

"Yep, fosho," Tristan replied as he got into his Lexus and brought his engine to life with his favorite rapper rapping through the speaker's, Pusha T Millions in the Ceiling.

"Good, now we finally have them together at once," the young head Federal Agent Patrick O'neal said as he caught the two infamous gangsta's Mitch and Tristan together out in the open public, on record of their surveillance at the same time, which was very rare that they've been seen together.

Mitch watched his big homie Tristan get into his car and pull off down the block. He looked up into the blue clear sky and smiled, not having a clue that the FEDS and Lieutenant Boxer had been watching their every move.

June 17th, 2014

9:15 AM

"Yo, ma, you ready to get up out of here for a while and start a new life?" Mitch asked Amber while he was holding his son Nasir. She was placing their packed bags by the door so the driver of the taxicab can put their belongings into the trunk of his taxi cab.

"Yeah, babe, I am but are you?" she asked back.

"Yeah, I'm most definitely am, kinda of nervous, though, since Chris said he might have a big career move for me out in New York City," Mitch said while putting his son down on the bed. Nasir started jumping up and down.

"Since you already have the plane tickets, what does the departure time say?" Amber asked in her sexy tone of voice.

"It says the plane takes off at 2:45 pm and it's only 9:15 in the morning," Mitch responded back. "But, baby, before we head to the airport, I need to make a couple of stops so I can collect some money and tell a few of the homies since I am going to be gone for a while."

Mitch walked over to Amber, grabbed her waist, and placed several kisses on her forehead as baby Nasir watched with a smile on his face.

"Okay baby, but please hurry and meet us at the airport. We will be waiting for you to join us," Amber said with such passion in her tone. She always wanted the best for her man.

"Okay baby, I promise I'll be careful and meet yall at the LAX airport once I'm finished," he grabbed his keys from the counter top and headed to the door.

Before Mitch, left he gave one last look at Amber who was there standing back holding their son and rubbing her ever growing belly with their second child. He gave her his fully pearly white smile, showing all of his teeth before closing the front door behind him.

"God, please bring that man back to me in one peace. I love him too much to lose him to these deadly streets."

Amber leaned against the door and looked at their son. He looked and acted just like his poppa Mitch who he was mimicking his every movement. Every time Nasir saw his poppa head to his office, he ran behind him with his toy laptop in hand, mimicking as if he was typing too. He loved to do the things as his father did and Mitch wasn't navie, he took notice and sat Nasir on his lap and he helped his poppa push keys on his keyboard.

11:14 AM

"Yo, murda, you got that cash for me?" Mitch asked Little Herm directly into the phone as he sat out front of his rock house pouring himself a shot of Henny that he had in the backseat along with a bag of ice.

"Yeah, I got that for you, loco. Here I come out now, give me a second so can rubberband it up," replied Little Herm as his words spoke through his bluetooth speakers in his car.

"Ight, bet," Mitch took a swig from his Henny cup and grabbed the half blunt that was sitting in his ashtray and gave fire to the tip.

"Damn i wonder where the hell is Tristan?" Mitch thought to himself. "He was supposed to meet up with me at my crib early this morning and help us pack, hmm…" he sat and thought to himself as he waited for Little Herm to walk out with his brown paper bag money.

The front door of the rock house opened with Little Herm walking out in a tank top with khaki shorts inline with his low top black and white Chucks. He was holding a brown paper bag filled with nothing but dead presidents all from the hands of that powder substance that corporate people loved. They called it nose candy. The powder, turned rock cocaine, crackheads couldn't get enough of. Sixty-five thousand cash in the brown paper bag was tossed into Mitch's lap when Herm walked up to Mitch's car. They gave each other daps.

"Take a cup and pour yourself some drank, there's some ice in the backseat. Take a break, murda, you well deserve it," Mitch said as he quickly skimmed through the cash that was mostly hundreds and fifty dollar bills with a few loose twenty's. "Just know, get it while you can because this lifestyle that we live there's really no way out and ending to it," Mitch said tossing Little Herm eight g's. "This yoour cut."

Little Herm caught the eight thousand that was bounded in a blue rubber band with his right hand.

"Don't spend all that shit on shoes, clothes, and jewelry, invest that whole 8 grand so it can double for you, crip," Mitch was trying to give game to his little homie just as his big homies did for him years back when he was first introduced to the gang and drugs at an early age of 11. "Learn from me, I'm an prime example. But, I'm about to go on vacation for a couple of months with the fam so hold the spot down and I'll keep in touch with you, crip," Mitch said pulling on his lit blunt before passing it to a young Herm who was sitting there soaking all the game that he could in like a sponge. "You seen Tristan? By the way, that fool was suppose to help me pack," Mitch said while trying to block the sun rays that were beaming directly at the two in his eyes.

"Nah, haven't seen him since the other day," shot back Little Herm.

"Well, he must be around here somewhere taking fades," Mitch said to himself as he sat back and enjoyed the last couple of hours he had left before he boarded the plane and start a new chapter towards his life.

Their silence was broken with the interruption of Mitch's phone ringing, playing the ringtone of the late rapper Dolla Closer to my Dreams. Tristan's name flashed across the screen.

"Yo, what up, loco? What happened to you? Thought you were gonna help us pack?" Mitch said into the phone receiver. "Where you at?"

"I'm parked right here behind you looking at y'all," replied Tristan who seemed to always appear out of nowhere and then disappear into thin air.

"Cool, you can drop me off at LAX so I can meet up with Amber," Mitch said.

"Yeah, fosho, I'll drop you off at the airport, hop in my whip," Tristan said.

"Bet," Mitch replied. "So you all good, Little Herm? You have everything you need while I'm gone?" Mitch asked.

"Yeah, I'm straight and if I need anything, I'll hook up with Tristan for some work. Have a good vacation, loco," he gave Mitch dap and a hug and he exited the car. He said what's up to Tristan and walked towards the front entrance of the rock house.

Mitch gathered all his belongings, grabbed his bottle of Henny, through the bag of ice onto the curb, locked his car up, and got into Tristan's Lexus.

"What's up, homie?" Where the fuck you was at this morning? I thought you were coming over this morning to help me pack some clothes?" said Mitch as he pulled out a swisher from his backpack along with his California green. "Here, want some?" he handed Tristan the bottle of Hennessy and a cup.

"I commend you, little homie, for sticking to your goals and dreams and silently knocking each one down while staying sucka free out here in a world full of lollipops," Tristan said as he poured himself a drink of that brown. "Just one more thing, I wanna tell you before I drop you off at the airport. Once you get to New York and become this big time author, don't forget to come back to the hood

246

and give back. Don't forget to come back and help change a young kid's life who is walking down the same path that we walked, little homie." That was the advice Tristan gave Mitch. They both clinked their cups of henny and made a toast to new beginnings and a promising future. They both took a swig.

Their moment of bonding and drinking was shortly interrupted by the ringing from Mitch's cell phone. It was Benny Cool, his publisher from the No Brakes Publishing Company.

"Hello, what's up, big bro?" Mitch answered.

"I can't call it... I just finished editing your debut book The Bust and everything is under way with perfect timing," he assured Mitch. "I guarantee you that this story is gonna be a best seller in less than eight months, mock my words, homie," he stated over the phone with confidence in his voice.

"Yeah, you honestly think so?" Mitch asked.

"Little bro, I'm telling you this story is like no other's that I came across."

"Yeah mane, I've put blood, tears, and bullets into this project for the last two years now," Mitch blatly said.

"Well, I was just calling to simply tell you that everything's on the right path and you should be hearing from me shortly," Benny Cool said. Mitch could hear the wind in the background, signaling that he was in traffic somewhere driving.

"Okay cool, keep me posted," said Mitch with a smile on his face.

"Who was that, murda?" Tristan asked while downing the last of his Henny.

"It was my publisher Benny Cool telling me that my book was being edited and about to be printed. He says that when eight months pass by, my book should be a best seller," Mitch said to Tristan.

"Yeah, thats dope," Tristan replied. He gave life to his engine and put his gear into drive. They pulled off from the block with the FEDS and Lieutenant Boxer on their trail.

"I'm going to get these bastards for once, finally, and they're both together," snickered Letiuntant Boxer as his protege Deputy Bradley was reaching for his walkie talkie. "We're gonna handle this one ourselves, no need for back up," Boxer said. It seemed as if the grim reaper had taken over his soul.

"We've got company, those same Sheriff's from yesterday are following our leads also," Federal Agent Banks said as he kept close, trailing Tristan and Mitch along with the dirty officers Boxer and Bradley.

2:15 PM

"So, you really ready for this transition, loco?" Tristan asked Mitch as he kept his eyes in the rearview mirror, noticing that they were being followed.

"Yeah, I'm ready for it. I have been working for this for the last two years now, going on," Mitch said with hope in his voice. "I wanna do something different now with my life. I wanna be able to show my little homies that it doesn't matter what circumstances you come from or the poverty of the ghettos. I wanna show my youngins that it doesn't matter what society declares you to be, if you work hard and treat your hobby like your job then one could move mountains.

"That's deep, cuz," Tristan said, his eyes never left the unmarked Taurus that was trailing them behind. "Yo cuz, the Turtle Squad behind us," Tristan started to pick up speed to separate the distance between the cars.

"Pick up the speed!" yelled Letiunant Boxer. "I don't wanna lose these cock suckers," he hissed as Deputy Bradley gave more gas as he turned on his flashing red and blue lights, signifying for them to pull over, putting them in a high speed chase.

All the adrenaline was suddenly suppressed from Mitch when the incoming call he was receiving read the name Amber across the screen. Mitch answered on the first ring.

"Where are you, baby? The plane takes off in thirty minutes and you're still not here," she said, worried while holding Nasir in her arms.

"I'm on my way now, baby, don't worry." He lied to her, knowing that the Turtle Squad was on their tail.

"Okay, well hurry up, I love you," she said with a smile.

"Love you too and I will see you in a minute," Mitch replied before hanging up.

"Fuck, cuz, should we pull over?" Mitch asked with concern.

"Fuck no, you know them pigs always had something against us and especially Boxer. You know we have bad history towards each other," Tristan said while trying to to speed up. "Aye cuz, look around under that seat for me, I dropped my cell phone under one of these seats," Tristan said.

Mitch began to look for his samsung cell phone.

"Yo, homie, check this out, I'm pretty sure you knew about this," he pulled two bricks of cocaine along with a brown Berretta from underneath his passenger seat.

"That shit ain't mine, cuz, I cleaned out and inspected my car the other day," Tristan pleaded the truth. "Shit, I bet it's someone who's working for that faggot ass Boxer trying to set us up," Tristan said, now with authority in his voice. "And, that's his bitch ass behind us," he said.

"Good, now we have them both together and hopefully, we don't lose them," said Federal Agent O'Neal.

"So, what's the plan? you know I have to get to the airport."

"Cuz, if we go down for this, you know what they'll try and throw at us," Tristan said in urgence as he raced down the 105 freeway towards the LAX airport. "Cuz, we're not gonna see the light of day for a long time. Just on gang enhancements alone carry 7 to 15 years," Tristan knew he wasn't gonna go back without a fight. "You know what we signed up for, cuz, this crip, remember?" said Tristan.

"We live by the gun, we die by the gun," Mitch said.

Mitch withdrew his 44. Cal Desert Eagle and began to bark at the corrupt Lieutenant Boxer and Deputy Bradley who had set them up for a down fall.

Boom boom boom! Flames and sparks rang from Mitch's eagle.

Pop pop pop! Tristan added with his 40 Cal.

"Fuck, they're shooting at us," Deputy Bradley said while ducking for cover. "You want me to call for backup now?" he asked Boxer.

"Fucking shoot back!" yelled Letiunant Boxer.

Deputy Bradley returned fire from his state issued 9mm while the FEDS were a couple cars back. They seen everything unfold in front of their eye's.

Tristan exited off the 105 freeway enroute to the famous L.A.X. airport.

"Fuck, cuz!" spat Tristan as the both of them started to hear the ghetto byrd starting to hover over in pursuit.

As Mitch sat there in disbelief, he thought to himself, "damn, when and where everything went bad at?"

"Damn, cuz, I'm supposed to be starting this new chapter in my life. I said that I was gonna retire and lay low for awhile while things die down, and we wasn't suppose to draw the attention from the law.

Mitch closed his eyes and thought about the bright future he had a head of him and the release of his debut fiction novel The Bust (Live By The Gun Die By The Gun). He envisioned that he had become a world-known prolific author while he slowly transitioned his lifestyle with new beginnings and his family with the new addition of their unborn son that was in Amber's womb. His dream came to an end when he overheard the loud sirens that was coming in closer and closer. All he could see was his son and Amber's face as he looked down at him clutching his 44. Cal Desert Eagle.

"We here, cuz," Tristan said as he pulled under the pathway to the airport. He lost the byrd in the unrestricted area.

"What now, cuz?" Mitch asked in frantic tone to Tristan.

"Freeze, freeze, put your hands up, y'all cock sucking monkeys!" Lieutenant Boxer yelled as he had his 357. pointed directly at Tristan's head.

He tried to open his driver door and make bail but he thought about it. He just sat there and closed his door, he knew the chase was over.

Everybody at the airport that day thought they were in a movie that was being filmed. Tourists and bystanders started pulling out their camera's and camcorders and started taking pictures and recording footage of Mitch and Tristan as they never seen nothing like this before.

"I should have killed yall niggers a long time ago when I had the chance," Boxer yelled through Tristan's driver window.

"Freeze, FBI!" Federal Agent Patrick O'neal yelled to both the corrupt cops with his gun drawn. They were trailing in the process of building a case against Mitch and his gang.

Finally arriving was the Channel 7 News with the anchorwoman Carolyn Tyler arriving with her camera crew directly across the sidewalk capturing it all.

"Put your guns down slowly and lay down," Agent O'neal instructed Boxer and Bradley.

"We're with yall, we are the Sheriff," Detective Bradley showed his badge.

"Get the fuck down, assholes, I don't give a fuck if yall are Sheriff's or not!" yelled Federal Agent O'Neal,

The two corrupt officers complied with his instructions. They looked around and saw they were greatly outnumbered by the FBI that took perimeter. Now more news stations were just arriving on scene.

"Now it's your turn also, assholes," O'Neal yelled to Tristan and Mitch who was clutching their firearms, still sitting in the car.

"So, what's it gonna be, loco? It's your call," Mitch said as he kept peeking through his rearview mirror, getting a good look at all the FBI Agents that were behind them,

All that Mitch could think about and see was the faces of Amber and his son Nasir who were waiting for him inside the airport, ready to board. Mitch opened his eye's, he still was clutching his 44. Cal Desert Eagle. He looked at his big homie Tristan and said, "fuck it, you right. We knew what we signed up for, this crip."

"Live By The Gun Die By The Gun. Love you, cuz," Mitch said as he swung his driver door open…

…. To Be Continued

Author's Note

Writing this urban tragedy novella was extremely important to me as a writer and black man coming from the streets of North Long Beach CA, an urban city with a reputation for murder and drugs. I want to be an example, like one of my favorite authors who inspired me through his body of work in film and the literary field. I wanted to also intentionally drop some valuable knowledge about this gang life that everyone may not be able to comprehend, but it's not for everyone to understand anyway.

"You see, I talk to the reader's but whisper to the streets" a quote by Jaquavis Coleman, is a statement that I now live by. I want my books to speak about the nightmares people have but are scared to talk about. I want to tell the stories that most cats are afraid to speak on due to their reputation, or perhaps even getting killed. I aim to show the good and the bad that comes along with

this street life and dealing with the effect of drugs and gang violence upon our very own communities.My books may draw a lot of controversy but hey that's what I'm built for. I want to have males that comes from nothing but hopelessness and poverty see that there is more to life than the streets and fast money.

If you've ever felt like your back was against the wall, or felt hopeless on the inside but your outward demeanor remained solid. When you are on your knees clutching your automatic pistol praying to the Lord for forgiveness of your sins….

This is for you, cause it doesn't matter what part of the world you come from, it doesn't matter what projects you come from. I am him, you are me and, **I AM THE STREETS**, One Love .
Raises Glass

-Stanley E. James II

NO BRAKES PUBLISHING

8760 S. BROADWAY

LOS ANGELES, CA. 90003

(323) 580-4339

NATURAL BORN KILLAZ

TO LIVE & DIE IN L.A.

BOY, I HAD ENOUGH

GIRL, I HAD ENOUGH

RATCHETVILLE

MIRANDA'S RIGHT

FULL OF LOVE

BONAFIDE CASH

LEADING JUSTICE

SLIPPERY WHEN WET

Visit the Instagram pages of CEO @terrywroten and Executive Publisher @bennycool_ for info regarding all of our newest updates & releases.